"Justly acclaimed for his lyrical, deadpan style by some of the giants of contemporary Irish literature, including Anne Enright and Colm Tóibín, Barrett offers an extraordinary debut that heralds a brutal yet alluring new voice in contemporary fiction."

—*Library Journal* (starred review)

"Many fiction writers are attracted to nonexistent but identifiable settings. Thomas Hardy created Wessex, Robert Musil transformed Austria-Hungary into Kakania, and in *Absalom, Absalom!* William Faulkner literally mapped his Yoknapatawpha County. At once Lafayette, Mississippi, and not Lafayette, Mississippi, Yoknapatawpha offered readers a familiar setting without the danger of their imaginations snagging on the join between reality and fiction. Colin Barrett confidently secures this same blend of familiarity and freedom with the first line of his debut short-story collection . . . his stories invite second readings that . . . seem to uncover sentences that weren't there the first time around. Chekhov once told his publisher that it isn't the business of a writer to answer questions, only to formulate them correctly. Throughout this extraordinary debut, but particularly in the excellent stories that bookend it, Colin Barrett is asking the right questions."

—*Guardian* (UK)

"A stunning debut . . . all seven tales converge towards one singular theme: the failure constantly lurking in the shadows of the human condition. The timeless nature of each story means this collection can—and will—be read many years from now."

—*Sunday Times* (UK)

"Barrett simply outwrites many of his peers with a chilling confidence that suggests there is far more beneath the surface than merely the viciously effective black humor."

—*Irish Times*, Fiction of the Year

"A sustained and brilliant performance by a young writer of remarkable talent, and confirmation that Colin is a writer of significance with something important to say."   —Short Story Ireland

"Raw and affecting . . . Barrett's use of language is powerful and surprising . . . These stories are moving and memorable."
—*Irish Independent*

"It isn't necessarily the job of fiction writers to explain our social landscape, but sometimes the best of them do. Colin Barrett's short, brutal collection of stories presents clearly and without sentimentality a picture of the young Irish small-town male, in his current crisis of hopelessness and alienation."   —*Irish Times*

"Superbly observed . . . Every sentence counts in these mesmerizing stories from an exciting literary author."   —*Irish Examiner*

"Sharp, edgy, heartrendingly provocative. Colin Barrett is a distinctive, exciting new voice out of Ireland."   —David Means

"*Young Skins* knocked me on my ass. It's moody, funny, vibrant, and vivid. It's beautifully compressed and unafraid to take a bruising or lyrical leap. Colin Barrett has, as they say, talent to burn, but I really hope he doesn't waste a drop."   —Sam Lipsyte

"Colin Barrett, like all great storytellers, has the ability to weave a broader chronicle of Ireland out of stories that remain intimate, powerful, and regional. Out of the local, the universal appears. He defines the many shades of the present time and suggests a compelling future. He is a writer to savor and look out for."
—Colum McCann

"Colin Barrett's sentences are lyrical and tough and smart, but there is something more here that makes him a really good writer. His stories are set in a familiar emotional landscape, but they give us endings that are new. What seems to be about sorrow and

us endings that are new. What seems to be about sorrow and foreboding turns into an adventure instead in the tender art of the unexpected."
—Anne Enright

"A writer of extraordinary gifts. I loved this compelling and utterly persuasive collection, the strongest debut I've read in some years."
—Joseph O'Connor

"How dare a debut writer be this good? *Young Skins* has all the hallmarks of an instant classic. Barrett's prose is exquisite but never rarefied. His characters—the damaged, the tenderhearted and the reckless—are driven by utterly human experiences of longing. His stories are a thump to the heart, a mainline surge to the core. His vision is sharp, his wit is sly, and the stories in this collection come alive with that ineffable thing: soul."
—Alison MacLeod

"Incredible. Human violence, beauty, brilliance of language—this book reminds you of the massive things you can do in short fiction."
—Evie Wyld

"A new fabulous and forensic voice to sing out Ireland's woes."
—Bernard MacLaverty

"Colin Barrett is a young man in the town of the short story, but it's fair to say he has the run of the place. This is a joyously fine collection, crackling with energy and verve, fit for the back pocket of anyone who loves a good story well told."
—Jon McGregor

"Should you be surprised that yet another superbly articulate and word-drunk writer has come out of Ireland? Perhaps not, but when that writer's work is as moving, as funny, as spectacularly evocative as *Young Skins*, you should be astonished, and amazed, and grateful. Some of the stories in this debut collection are amongst the best in the language. That a young writer possesses a talent this great is a cause for celebration, matched only by his ability to control and harness it. A minute after finishing this book I was itching to read Colin Barrett's next."
—Niall Griffiths

YOUNG SKINS

YOUNG SKINS

Colin Barrett

Black Cat
New York

Copyright © 2014 by Colin Barrett

All rights reserved. No part of this book may be reproduced in any form or by any electronic or mechanical means, including information storage and retrieval systems, without permission in writing from the publisher, except by a reviewer, who may quote brief passages in a review. Scanning, uploading, and electronic distribution of this book or the facilitation of such without the permission of the publisher is prohibited. Please purchase only authorized electronic editions, and do not participate in or encourage electronic piracy of copyrighted materials. Your support of the author's rights is appreciated. Any member of educational institutions wishing to photocopy part or all of the work for classroom use, or anthology, should send inquiries to Grove/ Atlantic, Inc., 154 West 14th Street, New York, NY 10011 or permissions@groveatlantic.com.

First published in Ireland in 2013 by Stinging Fly Press.

This edition published in Great Britain in 2014 by Jonathan Cape an imprint of Random House Group Limited.

Published simultaneously in Canada
Printed in the United States of America

ISBN 978-0-8021-2332-9
eISBN 978-0-8021-9210-3

Black Cat
an imprint of Grove/Atlantic, Inc.
154 West 14th Street
New York, NY 10011

Distributed by Publishers Group West

www.groveatlantic.com

15 16 17 18 19   10 9 8 7 6 5 4 3 2 1

Contents

YOUNG SKINS

THE CLANCY KID

My town is nowhere you have been, but you know its
ilk. A roundabout off a national road, an industrial estate,
a five-screen Cineplex, a century of pubs packed inside
the square mile of the town's limits. The Atlantic is near;
the gnarled jawbone of the coastline with its gull-infested
promontories is near. Summer evenings, and in the
manure-scented pastures of the satellite parishes the Zen
bovines lift their heads to contemplate the V8 howls of
the boy racers tearing through the back lanes.

I am young, and the young do not number many here,
but it is fair to say we have the run of the place.

It is Sunday. The weekend, that three-day festival of
attrition, is done. Sunday is the day of purgation and
redress; of tenderised brain cases and seesawing stomachs
and hollow pledges to never, ever get that twisted again.
A day you are happy to see slip by before it ever really
gets going.

It's well after 8 PM, though still bright out, the warm light infused with that happy kind of melancholy that attends a July evening in the West. I am sitting with Tug Cuniffe at a table in the alfresco smoking area of Dockery's pub. The smoking area is a narrow concrete courtyard to the building's rear, overlooking the town river. Midges tickle our scalps. A candy-stripe canvas awning extends on cantilevers, and now and then the awning ripples, sail-like, in the breeze.

Ours is the table nearest to the river, and it is soothing to listen to the radio static bristle of the rushing water. There are a dozen other people out here. We know most of them, at least to see, and they all know us. Tug is one many prefer to keep a tidy berth of. He's called Manchild behind his back. He is big and he is unpredictable, prone to fits of rage and temper tantrums. There are the pills he takes to keep himself on an even keel, but now and then, in a fit of contrariness or out of a sense of misguided self-confidence, he will abandon the medication. Sometimes he'll admit to the abandonment and sell me on his surplus of pills, but other times he'll say nothing.

Tug is odd, for he was bred in a family warped by grief, and was himself a manner of ghosteen; Tug's real name is Brendan, but he was the second Cuniffe boy named Brendan. The mother had a firstborn a couple of years before Tug, but that sliver of a child died at thirteen months old. And then came Tug. He was four when they first took him out to Glanbeigh cemetery, to lay flowers by a lonely blue slab with his own name etched upon it in fissured gilt.

I am hungover. Tug is not. He does not drink, which is a good thing. I'm nursing a pint, downing it so slowly it's already lost its fizz.

'How's the head, Jimmy?' Tug caws.

He is in a good mood, a good, good, good but edgy, edgy, edgy mood.

'Not so hot,' I admit.

'Was it Quillinan's Friday?'

'Quillinan's,' I say, 'then Shepherd's, then Fandango's. The same story Saturday.'

'The ride?' he inquires.

'Marlene Davey.'

'Gosh,' Tug says. 'Gosh, gosh, gosh.'

He worries his molars with his tongue.

Tug is twenty-four to my twenty-five, though he looks ten years older. As far as I'm aware, his virginity remains unshed. Back in our school days, the convent girls and all their mammies were goo-goo-eyed over Tug. He was a handsome lad, all up through his teens, but by sixteen had begun to pile on the pounds, and the pounds stuck. The weight gives him a lugubrious air; the management and conveyance of his bulk is an involved and sapping enterprise. He keeps his bonce shaved tight and wears dark baggy clothing, modelling his appearance after Brando in *Apocalypse Now*.

'Well, me and Marlene go back a ways,' I say.

Which is true. Marlene is the nearest thing I've had to a steady girlfriend—and if we've never quite been on we've never quite been off, either, even after Mark Cuculann got her pregnant last year. She had the baby, just after Christmas, a boy, and named him David for her dear departed da.

I ran into her in Fandango's on the Friday. There was the usual crowd; micro-minied girls on spike heels, explosively frizzed hair, spray-tan mahogany décolletage. There were donkey-necked boys in button-down tablecloth-pattern shirts, farmers' sons who wear their shirtsleeves rolled up past the elbows, as if at any moment they might be called upon to pull a calf out of a cow's steaming nethers. Fandango's was a hot box. Neon strobed and pulsed, dry ice fumed in the air. Libidinal bass juddered the windowless walls. I was sinking shots at the bar with Dessie Roberts when she crackled in my periphery. She'd already seen me and was swanning over. We exchanged bashful, familiar smiles, smiles that knew exactly what was coming.

There is the comfort of routine in our routine but also the mystery of that routine's persistence.

Marlene lives with her consenting, pragmatic mother, Angie, who even at three in the morning was up and sat at the kitchen table, placidly leafing through a TV listings magazine and supping a cold tea. She was happy to see me, Marlene's ma. She filled the kettle and asked if we wanted a cuppa. We demurred. She told us wee David was sound asleep upstairs, and be sure not to wake him. In Marlene's bedroom I bellyflopped onto the cool duvet; her childhood menagerie of stuffed animals was piled at the end of the bed. I was trying to recall the names of each button-eyed piglet and bunny as Marlene tugged my trousers down over my calves.

'Boopsy, Winnie, Flaps . . . Rupert?'

Now my calves are paltry things, measly lengths of pale, undefined muscle all scribbled with curly black hairs; their enduring ugliness startles me anytime I glimpse them in a mirror. But Marlene began to knead them gently with her fingers. She worked her way up to my thighs and hissed, 'Flip over.' You have to appreciate a girl who can encounter a pair of calves as unpleasant as mine and still want to get up on you.

'She's a nice one,' Tug says.

A fly lands on his head and mills in the stubble. Tug seems not to notice. I want to reach out and smack it.

'That she is,' I say, instead, and take another sup of my pint.

And just like that Marlene appears. This happens frequently in this town; incant a body's name and, lo, they appear. She comes through the double doors in cut-off jeans, sunglasses pushed up into her red ringlets, zestfully licking an ice-cream cone. She's wearing a canary-yellow belly top, the better to show off her stomach, aerobicised back to greyhound tautness since the baby. A sundial tattoo circumscribes her navel. Her eyes are verdigris, and if it wasn't for the acne scars worming across her cheeks, she'd be a beauty, my Marlene.

Mark Cuculann follows her in. Marlene sees me and gives a chin-jut in my direction; an acknowledgment, but a wary one; wary of the fact that Cuculann is there, that big Tug Cuniffe is by my side.

'There's Marlene,' Tug says.

'Uh huh.'

'So is she *with* the Cuculann fella then or what?'

I shrug my shoulders. They have a baby so it's only fair they play Mammy and Daddy; it's what they are. Whatever else she does or does not do with Cuculann is fine by me, I tell myself. I tell myself that if anything I should feel a measure of gratitude towards the lad, for taking the paternity bullet I dodged.

'She's looking fair sexy these days,' Tug says. 'You going to go over say hello?'

'I said hello enough Friday night.'

'Better off out of it alright, maybe,' Tug says.

I slide my palm over my pint like a lid and tap the rim with my fingers.

'D'you hear the latest about the Clancy kid?' Tug says after a lapse of silence.

'No,' I say.

'A farmer in Enniscorthy reckons he saw a lad matching the Clancy kid's description with, get this, two women, two women in their thirties. They stopped into a caff near where this farmer lives. He talked to one of them. Get this, she was—well, German, he reckons. Talked with a kind of Germanic accent, and they—she—was enquiring about when the Rosslare ferry was next off. Little blondie lad with them, little quiet blondie lad. That was a few weeks back though, only the farmer didn't put two and two together till after.'

'A Germanic accent,' I say.

'Yeah, yeah,' Tug says.

His eyebrows flare enthusiastically. The Clancy kid has become something of an obsession for Tug, though the wider interest has by now largely run its course.

Wayne Clancy, ten, a schoolboy out of Gurtlubber, Mayo, went missing three months back. He disappeared during a school excursion to Dublin. One moment he was standing with the rest of the Gurtlubber pupils and two teachers on a traffic island at a city-centre Y junction—the lights turning red, the traffic sighing to a halt, the crowd of boys and girls crossing the road— and then he was gone. At first the assumption was that wee Wayne had simply wandered off, disoriented by the big-city bustle, but it soon became apparent he was not just lost but missing. His disappearance haunted the front pages of the national papers for all of May. The established theory was that Wayne was snatched, either right at the Y junction or shortly after, by persons unknown. A national Garda hunt was launched, Ma and Da Clancy did the tearful on-camera appeals . . . but nothing happened, and nothing continued to happen. No boy, no body, no credible lead or line of enquiry could be unearthed.

Everyone's interest was piqued, for a while, given the proximity of Gurtlubber parish to our own town. But things go on, and bit by bit we began to care less and less.

Tug can't let the Clancy kid go. He can't resist the queasy hypotheticals such an open-ended story encourages. *What-ifs* proliferate like black flowers in the teeming muck of his imagination. Left unchecked he'll riff all evening about unmarked graves packed with lime, international rings of child traffickers, organ piracy, enforced cult initiation.

I tell him, lighten up.

'They could be lesbians,' Tug says. 'German lesbians. Who, you know, can't have a child. Can't get the fertilisation treatment, can't adopt. Maybe they got desperate.'

'Maybe,' I say.

'The Clancy kid looked Aryan. You know? Fair-haired, blue-eyed,' Tug says.

'All children look Aryan,' I say, irritated.

Marlene's laughter, a high insolent cackling, carries down the yard. She and Cuculann have joined another couple, Stephen Gallagher and Connie Reape. Cuculann is tall, underfed and rangy, like me; Marlene has a type. She is cackling away at something Gallagher has said. Everyone else, including Gallagher, looks abashed, but Marlene is laughing and batting Gallagher on the shoulder, as if pleading with him to stop being so hilarious.

'But it wouldn't be the worst end for the lad. It wouldn't be an end at all, really,' Tug says.

A waitress comes through the double doors, bearing a quartet of champagne flutes on a tray. Marlene waves her over and distributes the drinks, stem by stem, a strawberry impaled on the rim of each flute. Cuculann pays, and as Marlene drops the napkin that held her ice-cream cone onto the tray I catch the telltale twinkle on her ring finger.

'Wouldn't it not be?' Tug says.

He reaches over and drops his paw on my forearm, shakes it.

'Be fucking super, Tug,' I say.

He cringes at the snap in my voice. My mind, I want to say, has been enlisted in the pursuit of other woes, Tug,

8

and I can't be dealing with the endless ends of the Clancy kid right now.

'Oh,' Tug says.

He tucks his hand under the opposite armpit, like he's after catching a finger in a doorjamb.

'You're in a mood and it's—' he looks over, sniffs the air, '—it's Marlene. It's that loose cunt Marlene,' he says.

I make a disapproving click with my tongue. I jab my finger at him.

'I'm easy as the next man when it comes to getting his end away, but Tug, there's no need to be throwing round them terms.'

He leans back and his span thickens.

'I'll say whatever I want. About whoever I want.'

'You really are an enormous fucking child, aren't you?'

Tug grabs the sides of the table and I feel it shudder and float up from under me. I snatch my drink and lean back as the coasters go twirling off the edge. Tug sways and the table follows his sway, crashing against the concrete. People nearby yelp and jump back.

I daintily disembark from my stool, one foot then the other, keeping my eyes on Tug's eyes. His lips are hooked up into a sneer, his breathing fast and gurgled.

'I'm sorry, Tug,' I say.

His nostrils pucker and flare and pace themselves back to an even rhythm.

'That's alright,' he says, 'that's alright.'

He rubs a palm over the dented round of his skull and looks at the capsized table with an expression of broad mystification, like he had nothing to do with it.

'Come on,' I say, 'let's head.'

I drain the sudsy dregs of my pint and plant it on a nearby table.

Everyone backs away as we pass by, me in Tug's wake.

I know what they're thinking. Manchild gone mad again. Manchild throwing another fit. Oddball Manchild and his oddball mate Jimmy Devereux.

'Hi Marlene!' Tug says cheerfully as we trundle by her table.

Marlene is unfazeable as ever. Cuculann beside her is hunched and close-shouldered, braced for action.

'Well, big man,' Marlene says.

She looks at me.

'And not-so-big man.'

'Are congratulations in order?' I say.

I lift up the ends of her fingers, straightening them out for inspection. Marlene slips her hand from mine and covers it over with the other.

'Too late,' I chuckle, 'I saw it. Nice aul' hunk of rock.'

'It is,' Cuculann says.

'Very pretty alright,' Tug says.

I can feel him behind me, the looming proximity of all that mass, restored to my side and prepped to go ballistic at my word.

Marlene's bottom lip does something to the top, and she fixes me with a look that says: *pay attention.*

'Jimmy, I'm gone very happy,' she says. 'Now, please, fuck off.'

Outside Dockery's the evening sun is in its picturesque throes, the sky steeped in foamy reds and pinks. The breeze has grown teeth. Shards of glass crunch underfoot like gravel. There are cars parked in a line along the road, and one of them is the tiny, faded silver hatchback Cuculann boots around in. It sits there bald as an insult on the kerb, a wrinkled L-sticker pasted inside the windscreen.

'Look at the state of it,' I say.

I wallop the flat of my palm against the pockmarked bonnet.

Tug looks at me wonderingly.

'It's Cuculann's car,' I say.

'The thing's a lunchbox,' Tug says and laughs.

'A pitiful thing to be chauffeuring your bride-to-be around in,' I say.

'Awful, awful, awful,' Tug agrees.

'Tug, are you off your meds?' I say.

'No,' he grunts.

He places the palm of one huge hand on the hatch-back's roof and begins to experimentally rock the vehicle back and forth, the suspension squeaking in protest. Tug has never been a competent liar; his size, his physical advantage, means he's never needed to develop the ability to dissemble. You can always tell the truth, always say what you mean, if you're big enough.

'Be awful if you were to tip that thing onto its head,' I say.

'Easy,' Tug says.

He rocks and rocks the car until it is squeaking madly on its wheels and bouncing in place. It is parked at an angle, parallel to the lip of the kerb which is a couple of inches off the street, an angle that favours Tug. At just the right moment Tug bends down and digs his hands in under the springing hatchback's bed and pulls up with all his might. The wheels leave the kerb. For a moment the car hangs on its side in the air—I see the vasculature of blackened pipes that run along its underside—then Tug lurches forward and the hatchback goes over onto its roof with an enormous crunching sound. The passenger window shatters, the glass skittering in diamonds around our feet. The wheels judder in the air and Tug reaches out and stills the one closest.

'Well done, big man.'

Tug is puffing, his cheeks inflamed. He shrugs his shoulders. A car drifts by in the street. Child faces jostle in the rear window for a look at the overturned hatchback. An old codger ambles out of Dockery's, fitting and refitting a wilted porkpie hat onto his trembling head. His loosely knotted tie flaps at his flushed, corrugated face. The codger grins yellowishly.

'How are the men?' he says.

'Fucking super,' Tug says.

The codger salutes us and wanders right by the wrecked car, not seeming to notice it at all.

I look down and see, half in and half out of the shattered window, a brown leather handbag, its contents scattered in the gutter. There's wadded tissues, loose coins, crumpled sweet wrappers, a ballpoint pen, receipts, a roll-on stick of underarm antiperspirant, a gold-rimmed black cylinder of lipstick. I pick up the lipstick, unsnap its cap. I go to work on the passenger door. In bright red capitals I spell out my plea:

MARRY ME

'Shit,' Tug says, and clicks his jaw. 'Hardcore, Jimmy.'

I shrug and pocket the lipstick. I pick up all the other

things and put them in the handbag. I pass the bag through the broken window and tuck it into the passenger-seat footwell.

'Back to yours, big man?' I say.

'Sound,' Tug says.

Tug lives on the other side of the river, in Farrow Hill estate with his mam. Like Marlene, his da is gone, in the ground ten years now. Big Cuniffe's heart burst ushering yearling colts from a burning barn. Tug's mother is a sweet old ruin of an alcoholic who spends her days rationing gin on their ancient, spring-pocked settee, lost in TV and her dead. You say hello and she offers an agreeable but doubtful smile; half the time she has no idea if you're part of the programme she's engrossed in, a figment of memory, or actually there, a live person before her. Sometimes she'll call me Tug or Brendan, and she'll call Tug Jimmy. She'll call Tug by his father's name. Tug says there's no point correcting her. These distinctions matter less and less as she settles into her dotage.

We pit-stop at Carcetti's fast-foodery and chow down on chips as we take the towpath by the river. Slender reeds brush against one another as cleanly as freshly whetted blades. The wet shore-stone, black as coal, glints in its bed of algae. Crushed cans of Strongbow and Dutch Gold and Karpackie are buried in the mud like ancient artefacts. Thickets and thickets of midges waver in the air. They feast on the passing planets of our heads.

Up ahead a wooden bridge traverses the river.

The bridge is supposedly off limits. During a spring storm earlier this year a tree was swept downstream and collided with the bridge and there it still resides, the great gnarled brunt of the trunk rammed at an upward forty-five degree angle amid ruptured beams and splintered fence posts. The bridge sags in the middle but has not yet collapsed. Instead of removing the tree's corpse and fixing the bridge, the town council erected flimsy mesh fences at both shores and harshly worded signage threatening *a fine and risk of injury/death* to anyone attempting to cross.

But the fences have been trampled down, for the bridge is a handy shortcut to Farrow Hill and, despite the council warnings, is still regularly used by estaters like Tug to get in and out of town.

As we approach we see that there are three kids playing by the bridge: two very young girls and a slightly older boy. The girls look five or six, the boy nine, ten.

The boy has white hair—not blond, white. He's wearing a cotton vest dulled to taupe and a pair of shiny purple tracksuit bottoms, one leg ripped up to the knee. The girls are in grubby pink short-and-T-shirt combinations. The boy's face is decorated with what looks like tribal warpaint—a thumb-thick red-and-white stripe applied under each eye, and a black stripe running down his nose. He's wielding an aluminium rod—it could be a curtain rail, a crutch, the pole of a fishing net. One end of the rod is crimped into a point.

'What are you, an injun?' Tug asks him.

'I'm a king!' the boy sneers.

'What class of a weapon is that? A lance, a sword?' I say.

'It's a spear,' he says.

He stamps up along the flattened fence and hops back onto the towpath. He goes through a martial arts display: slashing the air with the rod then spinning it over his head, fluidly transferring it from one twisting hand to the other. He finishes by leaning forward on one knee and brandishing the crimped end of the rod at Tug's sternum.

'This is my bridge,' he says, baring his teeth.

'And what if we want to pass?' Tug says.

'Not if I don't say so!'

Tug proffers his crumpled bag of chips.

'We can pay our way. Chip, King?'

The boy reaches into the bag and takes a wadded handful of vinegar-soaked chips. He examines the clump, sniffs them, then peels the chips apart and divides them between the girls. The girls eat them quickly, one by one. They tilt their heads back and make convulsive swallowing movements with their necks, like baby chicks.

'Good little birdies,' the boy says, and pats each girl on the head.

They giggle to each other.

'You shouldn't take things from strangers,' Tug says.

'*I* gave them the chips,' the boy says, tapping his vested breast with his spear. 'What business do you have across the bridge?'

'We're looking for someone. A boy. A little blondie-haired fella,' Tug says, 'a little bit like you. He went away but nobody knows where.'

The boy knits his brow. He steps back up onto the fence and peers along the curvature of the river.

'There's no one like that here,' he says finally. 'I would've seen him. I'm the King, I see everything.'

'Well, we have to try,' Tug says.

Leave it be, Tug, I want to say, but I say nothing. So much of friendship is merely that: the saying of nothing in place of something.

I turn and take a quick look beyond the towpath, along the way we came. A hill leads up to the road and beyond that is the squat, ramshackle skyline of the town. I hear— or think I hear—sounds of distant commotion, shouting, and I picture Mark Cuculann outside Dockery's, raging at the inverted wreck of his car. Marlene will be by his side, arms folded, and I can envisage the look she'll be wearing, the verdigris glint of her narrow-lidded eyes, a smile flickering despite itself about the edges of her lips, lips painted the same shade as the proposal I scrawled for her on the passenger door. I feel for the cylinder of lipstick in my pocket, take it out, give it to one of the girls.

'More gifts,' I say. 'Well, let's get going then, Tug.'

Tug goes to step past the boy. The boy draws up the rod and jabs the crimped end into Tug's gut. Tug grasps the rod, twists it towards himself. He mock-gasps, and claws the air.

'You've killed me,' he croaks.

He staggers back, and folds his big creaking knees, and puddles downward, dropping face forwards flat into the grass, arse proffered to the sky like a supplicant.

'You've done it now,' I say.

I toe-nudge the fetal Tug in the ribs. He jiggles lifelessly. The boy steps forward, mimics my action, toeing the loaf of Tug's shoulder. The girls have gone silent.

'How are you going to explain this to your mammy?' I say.

The boy's eyes begin to brim, even as he tries to keep the jaw jutted.

'Ah, he's set to start weeping,' I say.

Tug, softhearted, can't stay dead. He sputters, raises his head, grins. He eyes the boy. He hoists himself up.

'Don't be teary now, wee man,' he says, 'I was dead but I'm raised again.'

He lumbers up over the fence and out onto the bridge and I follow.

'Goodbye King!' Tug shouts.

As I pass him the boy scowlingly studies us, arms folded, aluminium spear resting against his shoulder.

'If ye fall in there's nothing I can do,' he warns.

The bridge creaks beneath us. Halfway across, the thin gnarled branches of the dead tree spill over, reach like witches' fingers for our faces, and we have to press and swat them out of our way.

'So tell me, Tug,' I say.

'What?'

'Tell me more about the Clancy kid. About these German lesbians.'

And Tug begins to talk, to theorise, and I'm not really listening, but that's okay. As he babbles I take in the back of his bobbing head, the ridges and undulations of his shaven skull. I take in the deep vertical crease in the fat of his neck like a lipless grimace, and the mountainous span of his swaying shoulders. I think of the picture of the Clancy kid, scissored from a Sunday newspaper, that Tug keeps tacked to the cork board in his room. The picture is the famous, familiar one, a birthday-party snap, crêpe birthday crown snugged down over the Clancy kid's fair head, big smile revealing the heartbreaking buck teeth, eyes wide, lost in the happy transport of the instant. I think of Marlene. I think of her sprog, so close to being mine. I think of her sundial navel, her belly so taut I can lay her on her back and bounce coins off it. We all have things we won't let go of.

The beams of the crippled bridge warp and sing beneath us all the way over, and when we make it to the far shore and step back down onto solid earth, a surge of absurd gratitude flows through me. I reach out and pat Tug on the shoulder and turn to salute the boy king and his giggling girl entourage. But when I look back across the tumbling black turbulence of the water I see that the children are gone.

BAIT

This was a summer night about a thousand years ago and myself and my cousin Matteen Judge were driving round and round and round the deserted oval green of Grove Park estate, waiting to see what we would see. It was another bath of a summer's night, the moon low and full and hazed at the edges, as if the heat of the long day had thickened the medium of the air.

As was our custom, I manned the wheel while Matteen rode in rear, heaped like a flung coat in the far corner of the backseat. Nose glommed against the glass, he watched the rows of mute, single-storey houses slide by. There was a glaze on his forehead, a blue nauseated tinge to his pallor. Matteen was not well; inside, in his skull and chest, he was beset, I know, by that dolour of recollected feeling that can afflict any man who once loved some daffy yoke.

* * *

I knew something was up as soon as Matteen stepped out the door of his house. Cue case in hand, I could see it, the thick wade to his gait, like he was walking through setting concrete. At the window of the car, the chest of his T-shirt already clouded with sweat-sop, he looked at me as if he did not know me and said one word.

'Sarah.'

'What about her?'

'Spin us up round Grove Park,' he commanded.

Sarah Dignan. The daffy yoke Matteen once loved. Grove Park was where she was out of.

We'd been circling the estate for nigh on half an hour. Sometimes Matteen twitched at his trouser pocket, withdrew his phone, but he sent no message and made no call. I pictured nervous estate mothers eyeing us through the slit of their curtains.

Sarah's house Matteen knew well, as did I of course, and Matteen was making a particular effort to pay it no particular mind.

They had been barely together, really, Matteen and Sarah. The series of fragile public excursions that constituted their official relationship lasted barely a fortnight. They began in Bleak Woods, where the boys and girls too young or too poor for the clubs gathered most Fridays, in the carpark adjacent to the woods. The point of the nights in Bleak Woods was to get the shift. Music chugged from the open door of a parked car and there were tinnies and smokes as those to shift were determined and paired off. Shifting was a curiously bloodless, routinised ritual, involving lengthy arbitration by the friends of the prospective pairings, who, as in arranged marriages, did not so much as get to say hello until they were shoved into each other's arms and exhorted to take the dark walk into the maw of the woods. There, with that hello barely exchanged, each couple would find a sheltering bole to lean against or beneath, and commence their bodily negotiations.

Every lad wanted Sarah and it was Matteen got her. They went into the woods and when they came back he was pale with elation and, out of sight of the others, vomited with excitement.

I asked him what happened, how far did he get.

He just shook his head.

They went out on a few dates thereafter, Matteen with his hand gripped about Sarah's wrist, his eyes brimming with the terror-tinged delight of a man who has gotten exactly what he wants. Nobody knew what to say to them. Unanimously flummoxed were we, Matteen's pack, and envious. Matteen did not know what to say to Sarah either, and she, characteristically, said almost nothing. Soon enough, to our relief, it ended. Sarah euthanised it, proffered no explanation. Matteen, crushed, did not pursue one. Its demise was built into the thing's inception, was the way he considered it at first; good things do not last, blah, blah. That was a year ago. And Matteen was fine for a bit, clinging to this stoic philosophical read, but the loss was hitting him constitutionally now.

Matteen rode in back for in addition to his burdens of sentiment he suffered acutely from travel sickness; the gentlest spin, no matter how brief or clement the run, was enough to upset his inner equilibrium and turn his complexion oyster. The sickness was made worse in passenger, watching the world quail and judder at close quarters through the windscreen. The roomy seclusion of the backseat, part bed, part carriage, with his frame pitched nearly horizontal, was the only way Matteen could travel and not feel overwhelmingly ill. Hence this arrangement, and me as chauffeur.

On the seat beside Matteen was his cue case. The case was customised, a pebbled leather and stainless steel-clasped affair in which Matteen spirited about his disassembled cues.

We were usually elsewhere by now. We were usually in town. We had a routine and the routine was this: each night I picked Matteen up from his home and conveyed him to Quillinan's pub of Main Street, where Matteen made his money. He was the town's premier pool shooter, nightly dispatching several challengers. Matteen's reputation ensured a continuous supply of competitors, most of whom he had already beaten multiple times, all eager to stake a sum and watch in agonised reverence as he cleaned them out once more. Matteen was canny enough to lose now and then, purely to keep the flow of hopeful adversaries from petering out altogether, though he found it was those he destroyed most emphatically that were keenest to get back on the baize, to be destroyed all over again.

'Look, now,' he said, his voice drifting out of the back.

I squinted. The estate road was a trackless blot, but I saw them, the rakey flit of their darked-out shapes moving over the knoll. Girl shapes, one distinctly tall and one not, a pair.

'It's her,' I said.

'Of course it is,' said Matteen.

He said that and I thought I saw a flame, a flicker, but it was only her hair, high on her high head. Sarah Dignan was unnervingly tall for a girl, taller than me, clearing even Matteen who was six two. She was blonde, pale, unquestionably captivating in the face. Her beauty was anomalous, sprung as she was from an utterly mundane genetic lineage. Certainly there was no foresign, no presage of her beauty or her height, in her family, in her hair-covered pudding of a father and squat, rook-faced mother, nor in her older siblings. She was the youngest and only girl. Three older Dignan boys existed—broad, blunt and ugly. Temperamentwise, she was different too; the Dignan clan was country affable, ready to talk benign bullshit at the drop of a hat. Sarah was frosty, unpredictable, spoiled by the fact that attention never glossed over her; even when she tried to be reticent, she remained a relentless point of contention.

Given the incongruity in semblance and substance, theories concerning the Dignan girl's true origins and nature had regularly bubbled forth. Talk was Sarah was a foundling from Gypsy stock or an orphan from Chernobyl. That during her birth her umbilical cord tangled round her neck, asphyxiating and rendering her brain dead for five minutes, thirty minutes, an hour, but that she had inexplicably come back. That she suffered from Asperger's or ADHD or was bipolar. That she was either, by the textbook definitions, a moron, or possessed a genius-level IQ. That she had gone through puberty at six, hence her inordinate height.

'Who's with her?' I asked.

'Jenny Tierney,' Matteen confirmed. Jenny Tierney was Sarah's shadow, her tightest friend. Lookswise, Jenny had no chance against the hogging nimbus of Sarah's beauty, but I liked Jenny, with her pageboy haircut, freckles and prosaic legs. She had these gaps between her teeth.

'What are we to do?' I asked Matteen.

'Slow for them. We'll talk.'

This I did, crawling up along them, pig-flashing the lights to persuade them to linger. This they did. Matteen buzzed down his window.

'Hello creatures,' he said.

'Hello,' Sarah said. She was holding a naggin of vodka, a black straw sticking from it, handbag dangling from the other arm. Jenny had a naggin too.

'Haven't seen you in an age,' Matteen said.

'You look poorly,' Sarah said without actually looking at Matteen.

Matteen blinked his wet, heavy eyes. 'When don't I? What are you two up to tonight?' he asked. Jenny said, 'None of your business.'

'Well, that's true,' Matteen said.

Sarah shrugged.

'Trawling for cock,' Jenny said.

'Hah,' Matteen said hahlessly, 'well-well-well, we can furnish you with a lift, at least.'

'You heading into town?' Sarah asked.

'Where else?' Matteen said. He opened the door on his side, shuffled across the backseat to permit ingress. Sarah stepped instead around to the front of the car, opened the passenger door. She stooped in, smiled at me, addressed Matteen across the headrests.

'I'm not sitting with you.'

'Why's that?' Matteen croaked.

'Because you'll try something,' she said, then looked again at me, 'but Teddy is harmless.'

'Teddy is a gentleman,' Matteen said.

'Teddy is too afraid to be anything other than a gentleman,' Sarah said. She had a short skirt on. She lifted the hem, and slid one long leg after another into the footwell, careful neither to expose a square inch of knicker nor spill a drop of naggin. Her hairline dinted the rotting vinyl of the car's ceiling, necessitating a drawing down of her shoulders. She lifted her long-fingered hand into the vicinity of my head. I looked at the lined pink of her palm. She walloped me across the face, but playfully.

'Say thank you, Sarah,' she said.

'Thank you,' I said.

She giggled, and fixed me with her blue eyes, a calculated simper.

'Oof,' Matteen said in a mildly impressed voice.

Jenny bustled in beside Matteen.

'So Quillinan's it is, then?' Matteen said. 'Come watch me crucify a few?'

'Naaaaaawww,' Sarah said.

'Yeah,' Matteen said.

'Naaaaaawww,' Jenny said.

'You're in the car,' Matteen said, 'that's where the car's going.'

'You offered the lift,' Jenny said.

'You got in,' Matteen said, 'that's what passes for consent these days.'

*   *   *

Matteen led the way into Quillinan's, and I followed with the cue case, Sarah and Jenny behind. The irrelevantly elderly lined the bar, mostly fat men with dead wives, hefting pints into their bloated, drink-cudgelled faces. They did not seem to see us, certainly did not acknowledge us. We continued on into the pub's rear, into the adjoining extension where the pool table and a pile of young skins waited. There was a game ongoing. The in-situ players saw Matteen and raised their cues. Eyes caught sight of Sarah and Jenny and lads quickly retuned their postures, snapping into more assertive shapes.

I placed the cue case on a table and hurried back into the main pub to order our group a round of Cokes and ices—Matteen did not drink when he played. The girls did as girls do; panned the room, drew inscrutable con-clusions behind inviolable expressions, and click-heeled it to the sanctum of the women's toilets.

Matteen flipped locks. From the case's velveteen inte-rior he removed the split cue parts. He screwed one end into the other and worked the joint to a seamless squeak. He dabbed a speck of oil onto a muslin cloth and swabbed down the stick. There were a dozen lads around the table. Those who were to become that night's opponents rolled shoulders, flicked fingers by their sides.

Matteen addressed them.

'Five spot for a one-off game. Twenty for a best of three. Fifty for five. I am in no mood for fuckery,' he announced, the colour and conviction returned to his face, his voice assured, fluently cocky in this domain.

Brendan Timlin went first and lost his fiver in four minutes. Peter Duggan next. Best of three, gone in two rounds and eleven minutes. Doug Sweeney, best of three, gone in two rounds and fourteen minutes. So it went. An hour in and Matteen was up fifty-five quid even after the twelve Cokes he'd bought me, himself and the two girls.

The girls, meanwhile, reappeared from the jacks midway through Matteen's second game and took a table facing conspicuously away from the action. Jenny was leaning into Sarah's shoulder. The gaps in her teeth gleamed as she talked. Sarah was meditating on a noticeboard mounted on the far wall, a flock of expired circulars advertising manure storage solutions and faith-healing sessions tacked to it. The pinned circulars palpitated whenever a body went in or out of the pub's back door, and Sarah flinched with them, even though the breeze from outside was as warm as the air inside.

The body of boys teetered away from Jenny and Sarah, cramping itself tight around the pool table; it was respect of a kind, this physical relinquishment of a defined space to the girls. Only I broached that space, and did so with prompt servility, replenishing the girls' Cokes as required and then withdrawing. The girls produced their naggins from their handbags and liberally dosed each new glass of Coke with vodka. They did not turn their heads to the games, even as the spectators grew more rowdy and voluble. Matteen from time to time sauntered by their table, to casually disclose how smoothly things were running.

'Well, well done,' Sarah said.

'It's thrilling, isn't it?' Jenny said.

'These nights could go on forever,' Sarah said.

27

'And if they did, you'd be a millionaire, boy,' Jenny said.

'It pays, these nights,' Matteen said, his cue slanted against his shoulder like a marching rifle.

'And they just keep coming,' Jenny said, 'they just keep coming, and they go on for so long.'

Sarah smiled. A single vertical wrinkle-pleat appeared in the centre of her forehead as she considered Jenny's statement.

'It's the heat,' Sarah said, 'the heat in the air makes the night last longer. You ever hear about dead bodies in the Sahara, in its hottest extremes? The sun cures the skins; they don't rot. The heat preserves them, mummifies them of its own accord.'

'Is it that hot out there?' Matteen chuckled, nodding toward the back door, our town's staid concrete heart beyond.

'We're not used to it,' Jenny said.

'I am,' Sarah said, yawning. 'Where we going after, anyways?'

Matteen kept his reaction to Sarah's question tamped down tight, though even I felt a small thrill of approval.

'We'll see,' he said softly, and returned to the table.

'The woods,' Jenny said, 'the woods.'

Matteen walked past the money. He never touched the money. The defeated cast it onto the baize, crumpled notes and coins. It was me who snuffled the lucre up, who kept the running tally.

It was knocking on midnight when Nubbin Tansey, town tough and marginal felon, manifested on the premises. Matteen was up against Killian Weir as Tansey beelined our way, flanked by a couple of big units; ask the gods for henchmen and this is what they would send, twin slabbed stacks of the densest meat, their breezeblock brows unworried by any worm of cerebration. Tansey himself was short, at twenty already balding. He had gaping, thyroidal eyes, the broad skull and delicately tissued temples of a monk or convalescent. He had a tight T-shirt on, exposing veined biceps as tough and gnarled as raw root vegetables. He was chewing his own jaw and vibrating faintly in place, a bundle of seeping excess energies. He was likely on several substances.

'Judgeboy, the Judgeboy,' he said, slapping Matteen across his bent back as Matteen stooped for a shot. Unperturbed, Matteen maintained his low forward-bent stance, discharged his cue in a steady stroke. The central clot of stripes and solids unbunched, a swarm of balls scuffling thickly back from the cushions. The stripes   Matteen was always stripes—were hypnotic in their tumbling banded flicker. A stripe rolled into the top-left pocket, gone in a clean gulp, and the topside spheres slowed and stilled into a new arrangement on the green.

'Sweet,' Nubbin said, 'sweet, Judgeboy.'

'You'll be wanting a game, Tansey?'

'Maybe now,' Tansey said. 'Though I've a notion you'll beast me.'

Matteen raised his Coke, took a sip. The crowd was beginning to thin. The meeker lads were leaving while they could still leave unobtrusively.

'Can I apologise in advance?' Matteen said.

The girls had not yet turned around but he knew they were listening.

'Don't condescend,' Tansey said, and smacked his lips. He studied the table's stationary scatter of balls. He picked up the white, rotated it in his hand. Matteen cleared his throat. Tansey put the ball back in place. He pulled the cue from the grasp of the boy Killian. One of Tansey's goons loaded the coin slots. The potted balls churned down out of the table's gut. The goon put the triangle on the baize, clonkingly set the balls in place.

I heard the bark of chairlegs. Sarah and Jenny had twisted in the pool table's direction, interested now.

'C'mon so to fuck,' Tansey said.

'Be nice, Tansey,' Jenny said.

'I know you?' Tansey to Jenny.

Jenny shook her head. There was an amused uncowardly venom in her eyes, watching Tansey as Tansey's eyes crawled down her, then up Sarah.

'The Dignan girl. I know you, but. I know your brothers. You're attached to this set?' he said, nodding at Matteen and me.

'Tonight I am,' Sarah said.

'I know your brothers, Dignan. Christ, you're some diamond pulled from a coal bucket, you know that?'

'She knows that,' Matteen said, 'everyone knows that.'

'You're with him?' Tansey asked, eye rolling in Matteen's direction.

Sarah looked at Matteen. There is nothing worse than being pitied.

'Well, he's looped on you,' Tansey smiled, nodding again at Matteen, 'plain to see.'

'We playing or what?' Matteen said.

'Alright, alright. Go,' Tansey said, almost apologetically.

Matteen broke, potted a stripe from the break and then two more. His fourth shot he hit so viciously the stripe convulsed back up out of the pocket, spun confusedly on its own axis, and died into place a foot from the hole.

'You hit that one too well,' Tansey said.

'You want to come off into the night with us once I thrash your buck?' he said to Sarah.

'It doesn't work like that,' Sarah said.

Tansey turned, the cue's end rested on the toe of his boot, the cue tip stabbed up under his chin. He considered Sarah. There were beads of sweat all over him. Tansey was looking right into Sarah's face. Not many do, or can.

'Don't ask, don't get,' he smiled.

Then he turned and bent low to the table, planted the fingers of his leading hand on the baize and placed the stick wobblingly on a knuckle-ridge. Tansey seemed to be sincerely puzzling the shot, but when he fired forward the cue he drove the tip down and sliced a long rip through the cloth.

'Whoops,' he said, and stooped to shoot again. Again he gouged the baize.

'Ah would you just fuck off and leave us alone, Tansey,' Matteen said, paling in the face.

'There's no winning with some folk,' Tansey said.

He handed the cue back to the Killian boy.

'C'mon,' he said to Sarah, striding over to her and grabbing her hand. Tansey dragged her to her feet, but Sarah had a good foot on him. She loomed, she threw her head forward, down onto Tansey's chest. Tansey yelped like a pup. He stepped back from the tall girl. There was a dark blotch running from the chest of his T-shirt.

'Jesus, she bit him,' the Killian boy sniggered.

Tansey considered his wound, chin buried in his neck to see. He looked up at Sarah. He did not look upset, exactly.

Matteen glowered.

Tansey cupped the bit part of his chest.

'My titty,' he said.

Jenny got up, and now she grabbed Sarah's wrist.

'Let's go,' Jenny said, dragging Sarah out into the bar.

'Wait,' Matteen said, but the girls did not.

'Go on,' he said to me, 'get them back.'

'Me?'

'Catch up after them and attach yourself to the sole of one of them bitches' boots, like a good lad,' he said.

Matteen was clammy and pallid again. He reversed onto a bench, and leant his weight upon his cue.

'This thing ain't stopping,' Tansey said. The blotch was running, widening.

'Stitches,' said one of the big units with him, 'stitches and a tetanus shot.'

A rupture of laughter as I headed through to the bar, but the girls had already bolted from the premises.

I passed through the front door, into the street. It was warm out; warm and getting warmer, it seemed. We were enduring a marathon hot snap, a thirteen-day stretch of rainlessness unheard of in our otherwise perennially sodden clime. Water shortages bedevilled the farmsteads surrounding our town. Pasture had paled and browned and in the open country you could stand by the side of an empty road and hear the massed dry ticking of the bramble ditches that fringed the fields. Cows grouped in the shadow patch thrown by a lone dollop of cumulus and followed that patch as the cloud drifted across the sky. Dogs nuzzled the undersides of stones, seeking the moisture clinging there. In town, pensioners staggered in a sunstroked trance from street to street and tried to recall their destination.

Now even the nights were bringing little respite.

I thought I saw them drop beyond the hump of Main Street's hill. I followed. I heard laughter, the clop of unsteady feet, I saw flickers of hair and shuttering legs. I followed them down Dandon Street, close but with a steady gap. They were talking, though I could not make out the words. They were letting me follow. They turned and vanished down Ridgepool Lane. Moss speckled the phosphorescent plaster of the lane's walls. I felt its damp fur against my hand. When I emerged from the lane I looked left and right but could not see the girls. I went stock still, held my breath and in the weave of the breeze I picked up again their skeletal laughter. I foraged forward, and knew where they were going.

They were standing on the edge of the carpark of Bleak Woods, waiting. They were facing me but there was no light, the carpark was empty, and all I could make out were the disembodied ovals of what were their faces. The ovals floated in the dark and looked inchoate or on the verge of dissolution. Then they were turned from me and gone into the woods.

I had a horn by now, I'll admit. The horn had oriented itself upwards and was snagged in the waistband of my jocks, which acted as a kind of garrote sawing on the upper portion of the horn as I made my way into the trees. Obscenities, graphic recommendations, crowded my throat, but I did not let them out.

'Harmless,' I blurted, 'I'm harmless!'

And I was. Efficient deference was my singular mode of expression. I had never sought a status beyond that of sidekick or flunky, and in this way had achieved subtle indispensability. I was an adhesive creep to a degree, but Matteen needed me, as did the girls. I believed that. Who else would Matteen charge with pursuing these two into the night? Who else would these same girls permit to follow them into the woods?

There was no path. I moved from tree to tree and touched each trunk as I passed it. I had never been asked into these woods before. The trees felt like things that were alive and I had to remind myself that they were. Leaves depended from the fingerlings of branch ends and brushed my face like dry, frail-veined moths. I stumbled onward over stones, over monstrous hanks of rooted scrub. The smell of the woods in summer was heavy around me, and it stank of fucking.

They blindsided me, crashed into me from behind. I was on my face on the ground, in the dirt, and there was a measured vicious hailing of my ribs from either side. I got on my back and something shattered across my forehead, a wetness sliding all over my face, the precise fire of vodka seeping into however many cuts now decorated my skin. Then there was a weight on my chest and something squeezing straight down on my throat. I was looking up but I could see nothing through the burning wetness in my eyes. Consecutive wrenches at my thighs brought my pants down and the horn was out, sacked like a frowsy vagrant into the open.

I heard above me two-headed laughter and a voice, or voices:

Oh, Teddy,

> *Teddy,*

> > *Teddy,*　　　　　*we are*

> > > *We are going to*

> > *suck*

> > > *suck*

> > *the eyeballs!*　　*The eyeballs!*

> > > > *right out of*

> > *suck them!*

> > > *right out of your face.*

And then more laughter, and I could not tell who had spoken and who was laughing, and if it wasn't for the boot flat against my Adam's apple I would have begged go ahead girls, I would have begged do your worst.

THE MOON

Valentine Neary, senior bouncer at the Peacock Bar and Niteclub, had something in his teeth. His tongue probed along his upper row, where something wiry and prickly had snagged itself between bicuspids. With quick, successive jabs of his tongue-tip Val dislodged it. He swabbed the inside of his mouth with his pinkie and held it up to the yellow cave light. Val studied the thing adhering to the glistening pad of his finger. Once he realised what it was, he couldn't help but grin.

Boris, Val's right hand man, reversed out the side door tucked inside the club's double-doored entrance, bearing two pint glasses of Lucozade bunched with knuckles of ice.

'Credit that, Boris.'

'Credit what, boss?'

'I just pulled a wee length of pussy out of my gob.'

Boris searched Val's face, not quite catching the sense.

'Length of pussy . . . what?'

Val looked back down at his cocked pinkie, at the vagrant filament stuck there; it was a cunt hair, electric red, and it belonged to Martina Boran, the youngest and fairest daughter of Davy Boran, the Peacock Bar's proprietor.

'Nothing, lad.' Val smiled again, and with a flick of his fingers commended the hair to the North Mayo night.

'Ta Boris,' he said, taking his Lucozade.

'No problem, boss.'

Val could make out the noise of a vehicle approaching the turnoff. He took a gulp of Lucozade, swished it round his mouth before swallowing, and checked his watch. One thirty-three AM—the lights were going up in just over an hour but still they came, in a steady stream, discharged by taxis and minivans into the floodlit murk of the club's gravel parking lot, the boys and girls of Glanbeigh town and environs.

The Peacock got a young crowd. Over the years it had acquired a reputation for its selective—and selectively lenient—door policy; the sign tacked to the wall behind the ticket booth said YOU MUST BE OVER 21 TO ENTER, but it was well known that a certain laxity was permitted. Fanny frequently got in without ID as long as they'd dolled themselves up to the due degree. Lads were also expected to make an effort; proper shoes, a shirt, and to try the door in groups no bigger than three. The main rule was no drunks. Val had been on the door for eight years, and could read the drink in people's faces unerringly. Him and the rest of his crew—Boris and Mick and

Mossy—brooked no bullshit. Anyone with even a notion of acting the prick got the boot.

'Is busy, busy,' said Boris, nodding as the taxi pulled into the carpark. From it emerged four girls. Val and Boris took them in, the four bare-legged, in miniskirts and heels and tops devised from impressively inadequate swatches of material. Val squared his shoulders and cleared his throat. Not a one of them was near eighteen. As they approached the girls became quiet under the cool wattage of the bouncers' gaze.

'Evening, ladies. How are we all doing?'

'Alright.'

'Grand.'

'Super.'

Only one did not immediately answer Val's question, and she was the prettiest. She drew her pale face up, tucked a dangling tendril of dark hair behind her ear and narrowed her brown eyes.

'Well sweetlips?' Val said, and smiled.

'Not so bad, Val, no worse than yourself I'd say.'

So she knew him—but then most everyone in town did, at least by rep. Val couldn't quite stick a name to her, but nursed an inkling she might be a Devaney.

'Not long left in it tonight now, girls'—Val made a show of checking his wristwatch—'mightn't be worth your while, I'd say.'

Might-be Devaney grinned sourly, and sneaked a look off to the side of the building, where there was nothing but a couple of parked staff cars. She looked back at Val, kinked one perfectly etched eyebrow.

'Ah no, Val,' she said, 'we're still keen anyways.'

Val inclined his head and puffed out his cheeks, as if considering a revelatory piece of evidence, then stepped back and pulled open the door.

'In you go, girls. Enjoy.'

The others' faces lit up with relief.

'Ta Val!'

'Ta!'

'Cheers!'

Val only nodded, impassive. Might-be Devaney held his eye for a moment, then brushed silently past. Val took a sup of his Lucozade and plainly assessed the girls' behinds as they queued at the ticket booth. Hands stamped, they slipped one by one into the club's hammering, strobe-lit interior.

Back when he'd first encountered Martina Boran, she was just a kid, a mute, studious sixteen-year-old burdened with braces and baby fat. She'd sometimes drop in to the Peacock after school, when her father was tending bar in the lounge and Val was helping the floor staff set up for the evening run. Weekday afternoons in the bar were morgue quiet, the only regular customers a handful of the town's senior pissheads, intent on drinking through their pension money by a respectable hour. Davy loved to talk his daughters up—the eldest was a teacher in Naas, the middle one a radiographer in Bristol—and was no different with Martina.

'This one,' he'd say, grabbing the girl by her shapeless shoulders, 'is off to Trinity, boys. Medicine!'

Martina would only roll her eyes and sigh. She'd take a booth at the rear of the lounge, haul a brick-thick textbook out of her bag and bury her head in it for the next couple of hours, face set in an expression of miserable diligence, while her father happily pulled pints for the geriatrics pickling on their stools.

A couple of years passed. Martina seemed to drop off the radar altogether in her Leaving Cert year, and the next Val heard she was off at college; but in Galway, not Dublin, and doing Arts, not Medicine. She turned up again at the start of this summer, Davy having decided to put her to work in the Peacock on weekends. Now nineteen, Martina had grown up and into herself. First night on the job she showed up sporting a pair of knee-high leather boots and strategically gouged pink tights, hair dyed to a high orange flame, and a murderous glint in her eye that said the dowdy teenage bookworm of yesteryear was dead and gone.

Val found himself inventing excuses to hover in her vicinity. He'd lean against the edge of the bar as Martina stacked glasses into the washer, stall by a booth as she swabbed down tabletops sticky with spilled spirits. They traded banter, drolleries, exchanged knowing looks as the Saturday-night crowd heaved and swelled around them. One night a few weeks back Val offered her a lift home. Sequestered side by side in Val's Nissan in a shadowed corner of the parking lot, they talked pleasantly and meaninglessly for a few minutes, until Martina cut across whatever anecdote or observation Val was unspooling and asked him to stop acting the bollocks and do what it was he wanted to do. Val's knuckles tightened round the steering wheel as he mumbled something about not being sure what *that* was. Martina had only tutted, then shoved her hand decisively down the front of Val's trousers.

Since then, they'd been meeting up in a casual way a couple of times a week, usually on those evenings their work shifts coincided. Because he was almost thirty and she was a decade younger, because she was heading back to college at the end of summer, and because of the complications that would inevitably ensue should her da ever get wind of who, exactly, was ploughing the apple of his eye, Val had proposed that the thing between them be kept to themselves. It would serve no useful purpose to have their business broadcast about town.

It won't, Martina said.

The nightclub closed, the punters hounded out, Val went looking for Martina. She wasn't in the lounge, where the other bartenders were inverting stools and hoisting them onto tables. He figured she was up having a crafty smoke. He climbed the stairs to the first floor, moved past the Ladies and Gents and tried the fire exit at the end of the corridor.

Martina and Joan Doody, a stout, pleasant girl Val had rode a couple of times last Christmas, were standing outside, at the end of the small fenced balcony that overlooked the carpark. Their backs were turned to Val. They were sharing a smoke, but the smell—heady and herby—told Val it was no ordinary cigarette.

'Well,' said Val.

The girls startled and turned, Martina almost dropping the joint.

'Jesus, Val,' Martina said. She jutted her lips, expelled a flume of silver smoke.

'Hope that's medicinal,' Val said, and laughed. He then surprised both girls, surprised himself too, by casually forking his index and ring finger and gesturing for the roach.

'Cheers,' he said.

Val pinched the joint awkwardly between his fingers— it was already half gone—and jabbed its end into his pursed lips. He inhaled. The lit end brightened and stung his fingertips and the smoke tore at his throat.

'Hold it long as you can, Val,' Joan said, smiling.

Val tried counting to ten in his head, got as far as four then barked out a cough. His eyes sizzled with tears. He put his fist to his mouth, composed himself.

'Didn't know you partook, Val,' Martina said, taking the joint back from him.

'You've corrupted me now, girls.'

Val wondered if Martina knew that he and Joan once had a thing, but figured she didn't. It wasn't serious anyway, petered out equably, and Joan had since become reengaged to the lad she was having trouble with at the time. Val had a knack of staying on the right side of the women he slept with, a necessary skill when you operated in as tight a radius as Glanbeigh town. He looked down through the fence's honeycomb of wire.

'How're things faring out down there?' he said.

'The hangers-on are hanging in,' Martina said, and stepped forward, so she was standing shoulder to shoulder beside Val.

From their elevated niche, the three watched as the last of the night's crowd slowly dispersed. Girls huddled together rubbing their bare, goosefleshed arms. Boys stood alone with their chests out, fists wadded into pockets, glowering at the dark with thwarted, bloodshot eyes. Other boys and girls leant into one another, tangling arms, laughing conspicuously. Numbers were being carefully fingered into mobiles. Girls lingered on the threshold of taxi doors as boys extorted a final kiss and hug, the accompanying grope—open palm grazing the curve of a buttock—so brief as to be plausibly inadvertent. And certain pairings had already slipped away alone together, leaving their friends to make their own way home.

'Gobshites,' Martina said.

'He might have to go.'

'He being the drummer,' said Joan.

'Aye. Might be time for me to deal in his chips.'

'The lad on the course. Aiden.'

'Yep,' said Martina.

Val smiled.

Martina and Joan were lying side by side on a tartan blanket spread out on the grass in front of Val's Nissan. Val was leaning against the car's bumper, his tailbone knuckling the lip of the bonnet. His arms were folded across his chest, hands tucked pensively into his pits. They were on the bank of the Mule River, the car parked maybe ten feet from the water's edge, at the end of a sanded driveway leading down from the main road. The Peacock was a quarter mile back up along the road. It was gone five in the morning. Just before lockup Martina sent Val a text. FANCY A DRINK DOWN BY THE MULE AFTER. USUAL SPOT 15 MINS ;) Val left first, in his car, Martina following on foot, a bottle of rum filched from the supply room stuffed under her jacket, and Joan in tow.

The darkness was beginning to lift, but the girls, as Val looked down at them, remained blurry and indistinct in the gloom.

'And what's the fool done to warrant being got shot of?' Val said.

Silence. Martina made a noise, a sharp, catlike cringe. Joan responded with a nasal snicker. Val shifted his weight from one foot to the other, feeling rebuked for daring to intrude into the girls' flow.

'He's not a fool,' Martina said eventually. 'Well, not exactly. He's *nice*, Val, *nice*. But we've been going out five, six months now. And he's been on my tits all summer bugging me to head down to him or for him to come up here and hang, and . . . I just couldn't be arsed, either way.'

'So he's a nice buck, but not nice enough, or maybe too nice,' Joan opined sagely.

'It's like *just chill,* man, I'll see you when I see you, y'know,' said Martina.

'Oh, I hate when it's like that.'

'I don't even like his band. He's in a band and I don't even like them.'

'Well, relationships are . . . dicey propositions at the best of times,' said Joan and laughed. She must have surely figured out what the story was between himself and Martina by now, Val thought.

'He's so excitable. Laps at my neck, like a dog. *Pants*,' Martina said, sticking out her tongue and going *hah hah hah*. Joan started shrieking.

Val came up off the Nissan's bonnet and walked down to the edge of the water. He was keyed up, as he always was after a Saturday-night shift. Light from the main road threw a little illumination across the river's breadth, catching the innumerable dimples of the black waves as they pushed by.

'It's nice isn't it.' Martina was up and behind Val now. She pressed the mouth of the bottle of rum into his back, ran it over the notches of his spine.

'What?' said Val.

'The water. Looks nice. Moving along there, like a . . . well-trained creature.'

'You pissed?' said Val.

'Thought a man like you wouldn't need to ask that question,' she said.

'I can't see your face,' said Val.

'Kissy, kissy,' Joan groaned, supine on the tartan.

'Down here reminds me of Groningen,' Martina said.

'Groningan?' Val said.

'It's in Holland. I was there for a bit last summer with the crew from college, when we were doing Europe. We stayed in these wood cabins in a big park outside of the town, more like a forest really, with a pond and a bunch of swans living on it. At night we used to take mushrooms and go sit by the water and watch the swans glide around, and wait for old Father Time to swing by.'

'Father Time?' Val said.

'Father Time,' Martina said, and Val could hear the smile in her voice. 'He was this tramp, I guess, lived on the grounds apparently, though no one was sure where. He looked about two hundred years old and had this mountainous shaggy white beard that trailed down to his crotch. He used to tool around the woods at all hours on the oldest, creakiest bicycle you've ever seen. We'd be sitting there, out of our gourds, chilling with the swans at two in the morning, and then you'd hear the squeaking of the wheels and the clanking of the chain, and we'd start nudging each other and saying *here comes old Father Time*, laughing our asses off, and then he'd go whizzing by, and we'd shout and wave at him but he'd never stop or say anything, just give us the same wide-eyed spooky stare he'd always give us. He had a dog, a dinky little Jack Russell that'd come trotting along after him. The dog had a leash clipped to the collar around its neck, and it used to chase after the bike carrying the end of the leash bundled up between its jaws.'

'It's a clever dog can take itself for a walk like that,' Val said, watching as a pair of headlights approached and pulled in on the other side of the river. The far bank was relatively built up; there was a lit parking lot, a boardwalk and a wooden pier where a few townsfolk keep their rowboats and one-mast sailboats tethered.

'Look now,' he said.

Two men got out of the car. They were toting fishing rods and tackle boxes, and were dressed in waders, those shoulder-strapped, breast-high waterproof leggings. The pair plodded along the boardwalk, encumbered and

inelegant, like men in spacesuits. At the edge of the river-
bank, they checked their lines and stepped carefully out
into the current.

'You like this place, don't you, Val? You like everything
about it,' said Martina.

'That sounds like an accusation.'

'Not at all. Someone has to stay put, hold the fort.'

'You're not going anywhere that far.'

'Galway's not that far,' said Martina, 'but it might as
well be the moon for people like you.'

One of the fishermen drew his rod up over his shoulder
and pitched it forward in a fluid stroke. The baited hook
buried itself in the skin of the water.

The following Saturday, the first in September, Martina
blew off her final scheduled shift in the Peacock to head
back to Galway early. No valedictory fuck for Val, not
even a farewell text. It was a busy night. Val spent the
evening resisting the urge to check his messageless
mobile. Just before 2 AM, Mossy radioed in from the dance
floor. Val and Boris waded in through the crowd to find
two young lads going viciously at it beneath the DJ booth.
Mossy attempted to prise them apart and received a shot
to the kidneys from the taller one for his troubles. He
doubled over and went to ground. Without a word, Val
came up behind the tall kid and wrapped him in a head-
lock. The kid swung an arm back, trying to claw at Val's
face. Val pressed his forearm up into the kid's neck until
his knees obligingly buckled.

Later that night, at home, undressing for the shower, Val
realised the kid had got him after all. He touched the back

of his head. In the flesh behind his right ear were a row of narrow crescent indents where the kid had dug his nails in; the skin was broken but not bleeding. After his shower, Val walked into the kitchen in nothing but his boxers, secreting a trail of sloppy wet footprints onto the lino, and fished a bottle of beer from the bottom of the fridge. The moon, bright and engorged, shone down through the window above the sink. Val sat at the table for what seemed like a long time. After a while, he picked up his mobile.

The text he eventually sent Martina was so long, he had to dispatch it in four separate messages. He didn't think it likely that Martina would reply, or reply in any meaningful way. Still, he asked her how she was, was Galway as lively as ever, was she intent on dumping the drummer or was she going to give the lad another shot. Val said that he was sitting in his kecks in his kitchen at four in the morning with nothing but the usual shite having gone down at the Peacock, no change there and there likely never would be, and that no matter what had or had not happened between them he was looking forward to seeing her the next time she made it back from the moon.

STAND YOUR SKIN

Bat is hungover, Bat is late. At the rear of the Maxol service station he heels the kickstand of his Honda 150 and lets the cycle's chrome blue body slant beneath him until its weight is taken by the stand. Bat dismounts, pries off his helmet—black tinted visor, luminescent yellow Cobra decal pasted to the dome—and a scuzzy cascade of dark hair plummets free to his ass.

Bat makes for the station's restroom. The restroom is little bigger than a public telephone box. Its windowless confines contain a tiny sink and cracked mirror, a naked bulb and lidless shitter operated by a fitfully responsive flush handle. There is not a single sheaf of bog roll anywhere.

A big brown daddy-long-legs pedals airily in the sink basin. Bat watches the creature describe a flustered circle, trapped. He could palm-splat the thing out of existence but with a mindful sweep of his hand instead sends it unscathed over the rim.

Bat gathers his mane at the nape, slinks a blue elastic band from his wrist and fashions a ponytail, as Dungan, his supervisor, insists. Bat handles his hair delicately. Its dense length is crackly and stiff, an inextricable nest of flubs, snarls and knots, due to the infrequency with which Bat submits to a wash.

Bat's head hurts. He drank six beers on the roof of his house last night, which he does almost every night, now. The pain is a rooted throb, radiating outwards, like a skull-sized toothache, and his eyes mildly burn; working his contact lenses in this morning, he'd subjected his corneas to a prolonged and shaky-handed thumb-fucking. A distant, dental instrument drone fills his ears like fluid. Hangovers exacerbate Bat's tinnitus.

He runs the H and C taps. Saliva-temperatured and textured water splurge from both. He splashes his face and watches the water drip like glue from his chin.

Bat was never a good-looking lad, even before Tansey cracked his face in half, he knows that. His features are and always have been round and nubby, irremediably homely, exuding all the definition of a bowl of mashed-up spuds. His eyes, at least, are distinctive, though not necessarily in a good way; they are thick-lashed, purplishly-pupiled and primed glintingly wide. They suggest urgent, unseemly appeal. *You look constantly as if in want*, his old dear chided him all up through childhood. Even now she will occasionally snap at him—*what is it, Eamonn?*—apropos of nothing, Bat merely sitting there, watching TV or tuning his guitar or hand-rolling a ciggie for her.

Nothing, Bat will mutter.

You are a mutterer, Eamonn, the old dear will insist. *You always were,* she'll add, by way of implying she does not ascribe all blame for that to the boot to the face.

The boot to the face. Nubbin Tansey, may he rest in pieces. Munroe's chipper. Years gone now.

Bat jabs his cheek with his finger, pushes in. His jaw still clicks when he opens it wide enough.

Six separate operations, ninety-two percent articulation recovered and the brunt of the visible damage surgically effaced but for a couple of minute white divots in his left cheek, and a crooked droop to the mouth on that side. It's slight but distinct, the droop, a nipped outward twisting of the lip, an unhinging, that makes him look always a little gormless. Damage abides beneath the surface. Bat can feel by their feelinglessness those pockets of frozen muscle and inert tissue where the nerves in his face are blown for good.

Bat had been known as Bat for years, the nickname derived from his surname, Battigan, but after the boot and the droop a few smartarses took to calling him Sly, as in Sly Stallone. Sly didn't take, thank fuck; he was too entrenched in the town consciousness as Bat.

None but the old dear call him Eamonn now.

Bat palms more water onto his face, slaps his cheeks to get the blood shifting. The beers don't help of course, but the fact is the headaches come regardless, leadenly routine now. In addition there are the migraines, mercifully rarer though much more vicious, two-day-long blowouts of agonising snowblindness that at their worst put Bat whimpering and supine on the floor of his bedroom, a pound of wet cloth mashed into his eyesockets to staunch, however negligibly, the pain.

The doctors insist the head troubles have nothing to do with it, but Bat knows they are another bequeathal of the boot to the face.

He leaves the restroom and keys himself through the service door into the staff room. He deposits the bike helmet on the couch, unpeels his leather jacket, registers with a pulse of mortification the spicy whang peeling off his own hide.

On the staff-room counter he spies, amid a row of other items, a stick of women's roll-on; must be Tain's. He picks it up, worms his fist into each sleeve of his Maxol shirt and hastily kneads his pits with the spearminty-smelling stuff. As he places the roll-on back on the counter he notices a curled black hair adhering to the scented ball. He tweezes it off and flicks it to the floor.

Out front Dungan, the store manager, mans the main till.

Dungan is old. Fifties, sixties, whatever. He's the sole adult and authority figure in a work environment otherwise populated by belligerently indolent youngsters.

'Bat,' Dungan says.

'Yeah?'

'Take your particular timepiece. Wind the big hand forward fifteen minutes. Keep it there. You might show up on the dot once in your life.'

Humped above the cash register, Dungan resembles nothing so much as his own freshly revived corpse. His skin is loose and blanched, its pigmentation leached of some vital essence, and what remains of his thin grey hair is drawn in frailly distinct comb lines across his head, mortuary neat. His glasses are tinted, enshading the eyes. But you can tell Dungan is alive because the man is always snufflingly, sputteringly ill, his maladies minor but interminable; head colds, bronchial complaints and dermal eruptions hound him through the seasons' dims and magnifications.

'What needs doing?' Bat sighs.

Dungan looks over the rims of his glasses. The white of one eye is a blood-splatter of detonated capillaries.

'Sleeves. Sleeves, Bat. What did I say about sleeves?' He nods at Bat's arms. 'The tattoos can't be on display, lad. Plain black or white undershirts in future, please.'

'But everyone knows me,' Bat says.

'Professionalism is an end in itself,' Dungan opines. 'Now. There's six pallets of dry stock out back that need shelving and the rotisserie wants a scrub after that. We'll just have to try and keep you out of sight as much as we can.'

First break. Ten minutes. Bat is first out to the lot, peeling chicken-fat slicked marigolds from his hands. The lot is a three-quarters-enclosed concrete space done up to suggest a picnic area, where, the idea is, road-weary motorists can eat or stretch their limbs in what appears to Bat to be a rather bleak simulation of pastoral seclusion. There are rows of wooden tables and benches bolted into the cement (the obscenities carved into their lacquered surfaces only visible close up) and a ring-fenced aluminium wreck of a play area for children. Scruffy clots of weeds have grown up and died in the fistulas along the crumbling perimeter of the lot's paving. A mural painted onto the lot wall depicts a trio of cartoon rabbits in waistcoats and top hats capering against a field of green dotted with splotch-headed blue and red and yellow flowers. The untalented muralist had not been able to set the pupils of the rabbits' eyes into proper alignment, afflicting all three with various severities of cross-eye.

Bat perches atop the fat plastic lid of an empty skip, guzzles a Coke and regards the rabbits. The longer you look the more subtly crazed their expressions appear.

Presently Bat is joined by Tain Moonan and Rob 'Heg' Hegardy.

Tain is fifteen, Hegardy eighteen.

Both are summer recruits, and both will soon be finished up; Hegardy is returning to college in Dublin as a second-year computer science student and Tain will be heading into Junior Cert year in the local convent.

Hegardy ducks out into the morning air whistling a jaunty tune. He flashes a grin at Bat as he approaches, snaps a thin white spindle from his breastpocket and sketches an elaborate bow as he proffers what turns out to be a perfectly rolled joint.

'Nice,' Bat snorts.

'Let's start the morning and kill the day,' Hegardy says.

Tain rolls her eyes.

'Alright Tain,' Bat says.

Tain only grunts. She studies Hegardy frankly as he crooks the joint between his lips, sparks his lighter and with a forceful, fish-face sucking motion pipettes a trail of purple smoke-wisps into the air.

'Busy out front?' Bat asks. Tain and Heg are on fore-court duty.

'Quiet enough,' Hegardy says, and passes the joint to Bat. Hegardy has a foot in height on Bat, a handsome, olive-oil complexion inherited from his half-Iberian mother, the wingspan and streamlined solidity of an athlete though he takes no interest in sports, and a pretty wad of crinkly black hair, like a black lad's. He's about the most laid-back lad Bat has ever encountered; nothing fazes or riles him.

Tain hops onto the skip beside Bat, scoots over until she's right beside him. She picks up one of his marigold gloves and tugs it down over her hand. She jabs Bat with her elbow, nods at the joint.

'Pass it on,' she says.

Bat gives her his best look of grown-up disapproval.

'This'll stunt your growth, Missy.'

'Listen to the voice of experience,' Hegardy says.

Tain rolls her eyes, sneers but declines a retort. She pulls her peroxided hair out of her face. The roots are grown out, black as jet. Bat gives her the joint. She takes it with her yellow gloved hand. A brief toke and she is immediately seized by a bout of convulsive coughing. Hegardy's eyes pop in delight and his mouth gapes in a mute O of impending hilarity. He leans in close so Tain can see. She swings a sneaker at his crotch, Hegardy bouncing backwards on his heels to elude the effort.

'Handle your shit, Moonan,' Hegardy barks in an American drill-sergeant voice.

'It's handled, dickhead,' Tain says, holding her throat and working out a few clarifying grunts. Composure restored, she begins to pick absently at the small red nub of a zit on her chin.

Bat looks from Tain to Heg. For the past three months Bat has watched these two smile, joke, snark, preen and goad each other, with escalating intensity, up until three weekends ago, when the tone of their exchanges changed abruptly. For a few days the two were terse, even clumsy in each other's company. Now, while things have relaxed into their original rhythm somewhat, their interactions possess an edge, a spikiness, that was previously absent. This worries Bat. Though Bat likes Hegardy, he is pretty sure the lad did something—and may perhaps still be doing something—with the schoolgirl. Because he likes Hegardy, Bat has shied from pressing the lad upon the matter, lest Hegardy admit he has in fact committed something perilously close to, if not in fact, full statutory rape. (Which is what it would be. Bat looked it up. With no little trepidation he ventured to the town library and at one of the terminal computers, hunched forward and glancing compulsively over his shoulder, googled what he considered the pertinent terms.)

'When's your last day?' Bat asks.

'Not till Sunday next,' Hegardy says, 'but college starts pretty much straight the week after. So I'm going to have a couple of going-away pints in The Yellow Belly this Friday. Don't say you won't be there, Bat.'

'This Friday?' Bat says.

'This Friday.'

Caught off guard, Bat is too brain dead to temporise; no excuse presents itself through the double-daze of residual hangover and incipient dope high. Bat no longer socialises in town; no longer socialises full stop. He does not want to tell Hegardy this, though doubtless Hegardy has an inkling.

'We'll see,' Bat says.

Tain is inspecting Bat's arm on her side.

'This one's boss,' she says, dabbing a yellow finger upon Bat's kraken tattoo, etched in the hollow of his forearm. It depicts a green squidlike monstrosity emerging from a bowl of blue water circumscribed by a fringe of froth, an old-time ship with masts and sails encoiled within the creature's tentacles, about to be torn apart.

'Boss,' Bat says.

'Yeah,' Tain says. She traces a circle in the crook of his arm, and Bat feels a pinch as she nips with her fingers at his flesh.

'Ow.'

'You got good veins, Bat,' she says, then holds out her own arms for display. 'Big hardy cables of motherfuckers. You can't barely even see mine.'

Bat hesitates, leans in for a look. The down on Tain's arms glints in the morning light. Her skin is smooth and pale. Tain's right—her veins are barely there, detectable only as buried, granular traces of blue in the solid white of her flesh. There's a whiff of spearmint coming up out of her sleeve. Bat tries to ignore it.

'Why's that?' Bat says.

'Tain must have a condition,' Heg caws.

Tain ignores the sally.

'Look. Your veins are blue or green, whatever. But why's that, when your blood is red?' she says.

59

Bat thinks about this. 'That must be because of the lining or something. The veins' linings are blue and the blood runs red inside.'

'Blood ain't red,' Tain says. 'It turns red when it hits air, oxygenates. You know what colour it actually is?'

Bat shrugs. 'I'd be guessing, Tain,' he says.

'Bat's blood runs one shade,' Heg intones in a gravelly, film-trailer voice.

Bat looks from Tain to Heg and back.

'Black as night,' Tain growls in her version of the film-trailer voice.

Heg takes a final drag of the joint, drops it and sweeps it with his foot into a sewer grille, eliminating whatever tiny chance there might have been that Dungan would happen upon the incriminating butt and work out what it is they get up to out here—though that haggard bitch, as Tain refers to him, is nobody's idea of a deductive savant. Bat nods appreciatively. Heg is a thorough lad, cautious. Maybe he is not up to anything with Tain.

'Let's get back,' Heg says to Tain.

'Fucksake,' she mutters and pops herself off the skip. She heads in and Heg follows, turning at the last to catch Bat's eye.

'No, but come. It won't be the same otherwise.'

Dinner is boiled spuds, beans and frozen fish. Bat bolts his supper from a sideboard in the kitchen under the solemn surveillance of two bullet-headed eight-year-old boys. The boys are seated side by side by the opened back door, the old dear looming above them, wielding an electric razor and comb; the old dear cuts hair on the side, a home operation job, her clientele comprised mainly of the youngest offspring of her extended family.

Tonight's customers have the wide-spaced eyes and aggrieved, jutting mouths hereditary to the Minions. The Minions are cousins from the passed father's side, a clan notorious locally for its compulsive run-ins with the law and general ingenuity for petty civil dissension. Bad seeds, though Bat suspects the old dear is perversely proud of the association.

The old dear is shearing the boys simultaneously, in stages, not one after the other; she does the left side of one lad's head, then the other lad's left, then right/right, top/top and finally back/back. Kitchen towels are draped across the boys' shoulders and a tawny moat of chopped hair encircles their chairlegs. The back door is open so the old dear can smoke as she works, the draught escorting the smoke of her rollie out into the evening, away from the boys' lungs.

Above Bat's head a wall-mounted TV plays the Aussie soap *Home and Away*, but the boys' eyes do not leave Bat as he works at his dinner. The mane confuses little kids, who assume only women have long hair (and there's no woman in town with hair as long as Bat's). He's conscious also they may be eyeing the balky hydraulics of his jaw as he chews.

One of the boys slowly raises a hand, extends his forefinger and begins boring at a nostril, a movement that necessitates a slight shift in his posture.

'Don't be moving,' Bat says, 'or she'll have your lug off,' wrenching on one of his own earlobes for effect. 'She has a necklace of severed ears upstairs, made out of the lugs of little boys who wouldn't stay still.'

The lad stops boring but keeps his finger socketed in his nose. His eyes widen.

'That's not true,' the other lad puffs indignantly.

'Shut up the lot of you,' the old dear says, though of course she doesn't refute Bat's claim.

'What's your name?' Bat says to the lad who spoke.

'Trevor.'

A dim memory of a double christening, moons back, that Bat didn't go to. 'And that lad excavating his face beside you is JoJo, so.'

'Yeah,' Trevor says.

'And where's your mammy gone, Trevor?' Bat asks.

'The pub,' JoJo says.

'Is she out looking for a brother or sister for youse?' Bat says, grinning at the old dear as the boys look on, puzzled.

'Dearbhla,' the old dear sighs. 'Lord bless us and save us but you may not be yards off the mark there, Eamonn. HEADS DOWN,' she barks, and the Minion boys, perfectly in sync, fire their chins into their chests.

Bat smiles. They can be tough and they can be rough, but there's not a delinquent alive, budding or fully formed, the old dear can't crone into submission.

Before the roof and beers and bed, Bat hits the road. A night spin, deep into the countryside's emptinesses. The Honda is no power racer, but watching the dimpled macadam hurtle away beneath the monocular glare of his headlight, Bat feels he is moving too fast to exist; as he dips into and leans out of the crooks and curves of the road, he becomes the crooks and curves. A bristling silence hangs over the deep adjacent acres—the pastures, woodlands and hills sprawled out all around him. It goes up and up and up, the silence, and Bat can hear it, above even the hot scream of the engine.

His nerves are gently sparking by the time he lopes across the mossed asphalt shingles of the roof, cradling a sixpack. Bat plants his back against the chimney and drinks and drinks and waits for the moment the night becomes too cold, the air like a razor working itself to acuity against the strop of his arms; only then will he descend through the black square of his bedroom window.

The week rolls on. Friday night, the town centre. Bat in leathers, a pair of preliminary beers washed down to for-tify the nerves. It's been a while. He parks the Honda in an alley by the AIB branch. Shadowed figures linger out-side The Yellow Belly's entrance. Smokers. Bat approaches with his head lowered.

'Fuckin' Battigan. Bat,' a voice says, surprised.

'Man, Bat,' the other says.

'Lads,' Bat says. The lads are a bit younger than Bat; little brothers to those who would have been Bat's peers. One's a Connolly, spotty face like a dropped Bolognese, the other's a barrel-bodied, redheaded Duffy.

'Which Duffy are you?' Bat asks.

'Jamie,' the lad replies.

'Michael was in my class,' Bat says. 'We called him Scaldyballs.'

Connolly's face erupts in laughter. 'We call this cunt the same.'

'The ginger gene is dying out, so they say,' Bat informs Duffy, darkly.

Duffy braces his shoulders, looks at Connolly, who communicates something back with his eyes.

'What has you out anyway, Bat?' Connolly asks.

'Rob Hegardy's fucking-off-back-to-college do.'

'The brainboxes are off to brainbox land,' Connolly sighs, 'that time of year, I suppose.'

'Leaving us thick fucks to this dump,' Duffy scowls.

'Alright,' Bat says, stoppering the conversation. Inside he takes the couple of short steps up into the warm red heart of the bar. The main room is a long rectangle, half familiar faces eddying in its telescoped space. Some faces watch him; some don't.

Bat thinks: *I am here for Heg's fucking thing, so I'll go find Heg.*

Heg is at the farthest point at the rear of the bar. He is surrounded.

'Bat! Christ, good man!' Heg roars, and his companions' faces turn to take in Bat. Half a dozen lads Heg's age, and the same number in girls again. The girls; a dark-haired one stands by Heg. Cheekboned and smokily glowering, from her emanates a demeanour of regal peevishness, nose pinned up in the air. There is the briefest shift of light in her irises; she fixes Bat with the penetrating impersonality of a security camera. Bat drops his eyeline to the floor. He wants to hurl his body at her feet, repent his hideous pelt.

'Drink?' Bat squeaks, hoping Heg hears.

'C'mere . . . lads, you know this fuckin' legend of a man,' Heg loafs an arm across Bat's shoulders. He's had a few, Heg, his gaze lolling and sliding like syrup as he tries to fix upon Bat.

'Na na na na na na na na, BAT MAN!!!' Heg roars. Bat winces, shucks off the dead weight of Heg's arm.

'Pint, Heg?' he says.

Bat cuts a paddling diagonal through the crowd, riding up along the polished grain of the counter like a drowning man gaining the shore. He actually grips the counter. He orders two pints—one for himself, one for Heg—and downs the first in a single ferocious engorgement. He slams the empty onto the counter as a head rush ignites behind his eyes; he sees sparks and a wavelet of nausea migrates from the middle of his face into the pit of his stomach. Bat orders another pint.

When he turns, a girl who looks like Tain is facing him.

It is Tain, in makeup, in a dress. Bat's eyes drop, in a skimming horizontal, compiling fugitive impressions before he can restrain himself. The dress is a shiny kind of silvery red thing, a square of absent material exposing a section of Tain's chest. The dress's hem ends midway down her thighs. Tain's legs are bare. Bat has never seen Tain's legs before. Her knees are miraculously, mundanely kneelike—blunt, knobby and flushed scaldingly red, as if in embarrassment at so public an exposure.

Bat gets a grip, forces eye contact with the girl.

'I know, I know,' Tain says mournfully. She's blushing.

She has a parcel wrapped in silver paper under her arm.

'Present for himself?' Bat says.

Tain holds it out and rotates it assessingly in her grip.

'Pretty gay of me, I think.'

'Why would it be gay?'

'It's . . .' She glances across at the crowd surrounding Heg. 'Who's that one with him?'

'Don't know,' Bat says. 'His sister, maybe?'

'Fuck, no, that's not his sister. Are you being funny? I've seen his sister, she's a trainee vet in London. That's not his sister.'

The dimensions of the parcel and the way it bends in a U shape as Tain tortures it in her grip—Bat guesses it's a book. Bat is no reader. His eyesight has always been poor; the other derivation of his nickname. He wears contacts now but as a kid he suffered for years, believing the scumbled, dripping appearance of text on a page was simply how words appeared to everyone. It seemed perfectly in keeping with the variform sadism of classwork that you had to try to prise sense from the unintelligible fuzz of type on a page. The teachers thought him thick— and Bat was thick—but it was only when some of the other kids dubbed him booksniffer on account of how close he put his face to the page that he realised something was up.

'What you get him?' Bat means the book.

'Has anyone else got him anything?' she says, still craning towards the group.

'I got him nothing other than this pint,' Bat says. 'And I'd offer you one but you're too young.'

Tain swivels, with slow decisiveness, back to Bat. She makes a fist and wedges it against her hip. 'Christ sakes just get me a vodka and lime, Bat.'

'In a tick,' he murmurs, lowering his head and shouldering back into the crowd, brimming pint in either paw.

Forty minutes later and Bat has put away three drinks to the group's single round. Tain is several bodies beyond his left elbow, stuck making small talk to a plump boy in black. The lad keeps placing and replacing on his ear the wire frame of his glasses. Most of the crowd are from out of town; Heg's college mates, dropped down for the weekend. The dark beauty, as still and mute as a hologram, must be one of them too, though the rest of the party ignores her as she ignores them, even Heg; that she has deigned to stand in his proximity is the only suggestion of any association between them. But then, Bat, too, has largely kept his trap shut, his conversational contributions amounting to timed groans and dry whistles as one or another anecdote winds to its climax. They are all talking about and around college, the communal life they share there; the talk is an involved braid of in-jokes and contextual nuggets and back references. Bat feels doltish—too big, too bluntly dimensioned, a thickset golem hewn from the scrabbled, sodden dirt of Connaught. His jaw throbs— the teeth set into his jaw throb.

Heg is drunk, his expression adrift in some boggy territory between gloating and concussed. Abruptly the hologram substantiates itself—the tall beauty leans in and begins kissing Heg most vociferously on the mouth. He kind of writhes around in her grip. A girl with an overbite breaks into a braying laugh. Bat gently shoulders his way out of the group and wheels off towards the jacks. His nape bristles; he feels the drag, like a faint current, of someone's attention and turns. Tain scowling, in hot pursuit.

She still has the present, jammed down into her handbag.

'I feel like a wanker,' she says.

'Don't,' Bat says. 'Heg has us all just standing around like gobshites.'

A hand on Bat's shoulder. He flinches.

'Fuck me, man, how's it going?'

Bat's grip tenses around a phantom pint. He gulps. But it's only Luke Minion. As it goes Luke is one of the more congenial strands of that brood of cousins. Luke has always had time for Bat; was witness to the boot to the face.

'Well, Luke.'

'It's been an age, lad.'

'Yeah.'

'Who's this?' Minion asks of Tain, an amused curl to the lip.

'I work with her. Tain. This is Luke.'

'You're still out with the Maxol crowd.'

'It's a living,' Bat says.

'It is,' Minion says through his teeth. He runs a hand through his crow-coloured cowlick of a widow's peak. Most of the Minions are stocky and solidly hipped. Luke is rangy, with clear grey eyes. Last Bat heard the man was running up mountains; there was talk of a sponsored tackle of Kilimanjaro. It never happened. Before that Luke had been living in a mobile home on the farthest acre of his family's farmplot. He'd had a Czechoslovakian girl and a baba stowed away there for a while, but one day the pair woke up and the baba was dead.

'What you at these days?'

Minion's eyebrows rise, 'Bits and pieces.'

'In the Minion fashion,' Bat says, hearing the old dear in his tone.

'This guy,' Luke says to Tain. 'You ever hear tell of how he wound up with that face?'

Tain looks to Bat.

Bat wonders if she can read the total misery in his visage.

'No,' she says brightly, looking more like a child, in her densely daubed mask of makeup, than ever before.

'Yeah,' Luke says, 'sure you're only a young one.'

'Hitting the jacks,' Bat says, his throat going tight, like he's just swallowed a plum gourd.

The nausea has resurfaced in the other direction, a roiling ball of unpleasantness bubbling out of his gut. His mouth waters, and he tastes a flash of blood. He wipes his mouth with his sleeve. His head is sore; his head is always sore. The headaches tune down to a vestige, but they never truly go.

The drinking doesn't help, Bat thinks, *but it does help*.

As he slams open a cubicle door the possibility of throwing up seems fragilely close. He gropes the door shut behind him. A pitifully loud retch doubles him over; nothing follows but a gutty hock, a hot trickle of bile. Bat retches until it plops from his lips into the jacks' waiting mouth.

There in the cubicle, unbidden, floats up the remnant of a dream; a recurring dream, Bat knows intuitively, though this is the first time he has consciously recalled recalling it. The dream remnant is merely this, like a random, unfinished scene from a film: Bat is Bat, but in a different body. A Dungan-like body, wasted and bowlegged, older perhaps, though perhaps not. Certainly frailer, flimsier, and he, dream-Bat, is walking around what must be this town. It's just a street, an undistinguished strip of concrete paving flanked by generic buildings—and he's wearing a mustard-seed suit. That's what his mother—in the dream—calls the suit. The suit does not fit. It's several sizes too large and the superfluous material billows and flumps comically around his limbs. And in the dream all Bat is doing is walking around and around and crying and crying and somewhere to the back of him—he can't precisely tell—his old dear's voice pursues him like a vindictive raincloud, saying *change the medication, change the medication*.

How long has he been having this fucking dream, he wonders?

And then his thoughts turn to the boot to the face; the last thing Bat himself recalls of that night was staggering through the door of Munroe's takeaway with a hunger in his belly, his head down and headphones in, music blaring and scrolling through his playlist to see what song was cued up next. He woke up in hospital. The culprit was a five-foot-two sparkplug went by Nubbin Tansey, and Luke Minion was there, saw it all unfold.

And now Tain is outside. Tain is on a stool by the bar, waiting for Bat to return. Bat squinches closed his eyes.

How long have I been having this fucking dream?

Tain is on a stool and Minion, expert bar-grift, has inveigled her into buying him a drink—the first she's ever ordered in a bar. The barlad didn't look at her twice as she put in the round. It makes Tain feel pathetically proud of herself. She's on her fourth vodka and lime and has no more money. The odour of limes—spiked and soured by the gelid see-through spirit—is all she can smell. She's watching Minion—the lad finicks with his stool, skims his palm round the lip of the seat like he's searching for the sweet spot. Finally he hoists himself into position. He looks at her and launches in.

'It must've been up on the heels of four on a Saturday morning, Munroe's being one of the few eateries still open at that hour so it was fairly packed. I was queuing at the counter, hangover already coming on, waiting on a kebab and batter burger. Nubbin Tansey was up on one of the tabletops, making a holy fucking show of himself. Now Tansey was a shortarse but he was built through; physique of a jockey on steroids. He was well oiled, as we all were, looking wild and dishevelled, his shirt hanging off him, buttons all burst off, Doc Martens scuffing the Formica as he whelped out a furious jig. His boys were crowing him on—there were five or six of them, big rowdy units—and the Turkish lads behind the counter weren't going to risk stepping in, though good old Saleem, the manager, was threatening to call the pigs if Tansey didn't get the fuck down fairly lively. Tansey, bald since seventeen to go with the height deficiency, was amped up, face gone red and every veineen in his skull popping, a solid wall of perspiration coming right off him and fizzing in the fluorescence as he jigged and jigged. Nervous little cheers coming up from all corners of the takeaway, hoping he'd stop. Then Tansey started out with these karate moves, firing the legs out and chop sockying the air, which brought up further cheers. He was moving fair graceful for a man as scuttered as he was. And then he stops, a tacky sling of spit flapping from his chin. He wipes the spit and says to the boys, 'I'm taking the head, THE HEAD, off the next cunt comes through that door,' and points at the entrance, a good six feet away from the edge of the tabletop he's prancing on. Another cheer at Tansey's declaration, though this time only from his boys. And for a while that was that, there was this little spell, thirty seconds, where everything got quiet, even Tanscy seemed to be winding down. He'd gone into a squat and was sharing a private chuckle with one of his boys when the doorbell jingles, the jingle letting everyone know there's a body coming through, and I saw the shock of jet hair, the leather jacket and Bat's battered runners. Not a chance to say nothing. Not that I believed, I suppose, that Tansey was actually going to follow through on his boast; shite talk and no follow through, I had it diagnosed. But the bell jingles, and in steps Bat, oblivious that he was the next cunt, elected by fate, and without a hesitation, without even stopping to see who he was going for,

Tansey up and leapt. It was some fuck of a leap, credit to the lad, his leg straight as a rod leading his body, clearing that six feet and stoving slap bang into the side of Bat's head. Cleanest connect of a jaw you'll ever see, Bat sent flying like a rag doll. Spun and flung. He smacked the wall and bounced back up off the floor and then down again in a buckled heap. And Tansey—Tansey landed perfectly on his feet. Some young wan had let out a scream but now there was no noise except for Tansey's breathing. His eyes were lit, in a marvel at what he'd done. No noise but the air heaving in and out of him, and Bat facedown in a sprawl of hair and blood. Every last cunt there must've thought he was dead. I did.'

'Nubbin Tansey,' Tain says. 'I don't know him.'

'You wouldn't,' Minion says. He was actually inspecting his nails now. 'He's dead. Been dead three years.'

'How'd he die?'

'Rigged a rope round the crossbeam in his folks' shed and—' Minion takes his feet up off the floor. He hitches each shoe into the bottom rung of his stool and leans forward until the stool tips over. He fires out the feet to land standing, twists and catches the stool before it clatters to the ground.

'Jeez,' Tain said. She has placed the silver parcel flat on the counter and is now steadily picking away at a bit of sellotape on the wrapping.

'No, no,' Minion insists. 'None of that. Tansey—he was one of those ones with nothing good in him. He was a fucking headcase. Paranoid, devious, a temper he couldn't turn down. Would kick the shit out of you at the drop of a hat—and I mean *you*. The mother of his kid wouldn't let him see the baby—he beat her to a pulp, cracked a bottle over her skull. He was one of them couldn't stand being in his own skin, and couldn't stand the rest of us neither.'

Tain takes a sip of her vodka and lime.

'Saddening?' Luke Minion says.

Tain bunches her lips together, shakes her head.

'Did Bat not get the guards on him?'

'The mother wanted to, and half the Minion clan wanted to kill the lad, they were just waiting on Bat's say-so. But Bat never said nothing, didn't even press charges. Tansey was one of them ones in and out of the county court every other day anyway—another stint wouldn't have bothered him. There was a manner of settlement—the Tanseys footed the bill for the surgery Bat had to have after. But that was it, as far as retribution went, on Bat's side. You're his friend, aren't you?'

'Yes,' Tain says.

'You know him, then. I used to pick on him a lot when we were kids. We all did. And if I wanted an excuse I could say he was the type that asked for it, or didn't know how not to ask for it. Slap him in the face nine times and he'd come right back for number ten.'

There's a silence. Luke turns out from the bar, angles a sidling look at Tain.

'What age are you?' Luke says.

'Eighteen.'

'You with Bat?' he says, and flicks a brutal gesture with one hand.

Tain colours. 'It's . . . it's nothing like that.'

'Well,' Luke drawls, 'we could go somewhere and have you just sit on my face for an hour?'

'What the fuck,' Tain blurts, then bursts out laughing.

Minion cackles.

'Just a suggestion,' he says and offers a trivially unfussed shrug of the shoulder.

Tain looks towards Heg's party. The dark beauty has collapsed in a despicably graceful heap on Rob, who can't help but look like the smuggest prick in the world.

'That fella then, is it?' Minion said.

'Huh,' Tain says.

'That curly-headed faggot with the ride welded to him. He's what has you doleful. I can see.'

He has his hand now on her thigh, up under the hem and on the bare flesh.

'If it helps, this'll be nothing other than meaningless,' he says.

So when Bat emerges from the jacks he stomps back towards Tain and this is what he sees; Minion, wrapped round her, mouth on hers. She's rolling her shoulders in tandem to Minion's impassioned flinchings, though there's something mechanistic and barely controlled in her reciprocation. It looks coercive, Bat thinks sadly, but with a kind of concluding satisfaction. Tonight was a mistake, emphatically so, and this display of frankly felonious lechery is a fitting cap. Bat waggles the big stupid shovels of his hands.

Last words present themselves.

He could say: *Bye Heg, thanks for nothing, hope you and your fucking college buddies got a good laugh out of tonight.*

He could say: *Why Tain, why be that fucking pathetic, you're cleverer than that, and you're cleverer than Heg too.*

But he'll say nothing, of course. His jaw throbs. It throbs with nothing. All he wants is a drink, but he can get that at home.

Bat puts the head down, hair enfolding him like a screen, and leaves the humans to the humans.

In the lane where his bike is parked Bat runs a hand round the inside of the helmet to make sure no kids have pissed in it or stuck it with chewing gum. The helmet's grotty foam lining slips tight as a callipers round his head. Ignition and Bat takes a moment to listen: the engine's rumble, overlapping with its own echo, crashes like surf back off the lane's narrow walls.

On the way home he zips by the Maxol station and for the fuck of it he does a lap of the premises. He slows to a stop out back. In the scanty, grained moonlight and with his iffy sight he can still just about decipher the trio of painted rabbits on the wall. He thinks of the stoic mania of their botched gazes and it is unnerving, now, to consider them presiding over the bleak emptiness of the lot, night after night after night.

Bat realises he is silently mouthing Tain's name over and over.

At home the old dear is in the dark, in the sitting room, TV light the only illumination. In repose, half asleep, her face looks embalmed. It is not a restful expression. She has a wool blanket clutched up to her throat.

'I can smell you from the hallway,' she says.

'Thanks, Ma,' Bat says. In the kitchen he pulls a six-pack from the fridge.

He cracks one open, wolfs it down. Around him Bat can hear the incessant creaking of the house fixtures, like a field of ice coming apart in increments. A draught runs from several accesses and converges in the kitchen, frigidly whistling by Bat's ear. He hears the fretful scrawlings of rats behind the walls, under the pipes. . . .

'How was the town?' the old dear asks.

'Fine,' Bat groans.

'I bet it was.'

'Who'd you see?'

'Luke Minion. Couple of work folk. Hegardy, the Moonan girl. Saw Peter Donnelly's youngest, Danny Duffy. '

'Sounds like they were all out, so.'

When Bat does not answer she says, 'Was it alright?'

'I survived,' Bat says.

The *pksssh* of a can's tab getting popped. The old dear shifts in her seat. She listens to her son's effortful ascent, the lumbering clop of each step up the squeaking stairs and then the succession of fainter percussive pulses travelling the sitting-room ceiling as he moves from the landing into, and then across, his bedroom. She's sure she can hear the shunt of the window and then he is out and up onto the roof; though she must make this assumption on faith.

She has dreams of him falling, of Eamonn letting himself fall. She has dreams of his bike leaving the road, his body a red rent along the macadam of some bleak country lane and the massive, settling silence afterwards. This is what a mother must do: preemptively conjure the worst-case scenarios in order to avert them. She never considered or foresaw that little shit Nubbin Tansey and his boot, and *he* happened. She cannot make that mistake again.

There is a part of her that hates her son, the enormous, fatiguing fragility of him.

She watches the TV and listens, without intentionally listening, for the creak and thud of his return through the window. On the TV her favourite host and his guests. Entire passages of conversation slip by. She falls asleep and jolts abruptly to, not knowing she's been asleep.

The TV screen is extinguished, a minute blue dot levitating in its dark centre. The draught whistles, far above her, through the black; there is no noise and it is dark everywhere. For a long moment she does not know who she is, or where she is. When it comes back to her, she calls out for her son.

CALM WITH HORSES

Dympna told Arm to stay in the car while Dympna gave Fannigan a chance to plead his case. This wasn't the way it usually went, but Arm nodded *okay*. Arm watched Dympna stalk up the lawn and politely hammer on the front door of the council house Fannigan shared with his mother. Eventually Dympna was let inside.

Arm slid in his earphones and sank in the passenger seat. The car was originally Dympna's Uncle Hector's, a battered cranberry Corolla Dympna dubbed the shitbox, its interior upholstered in tan vinyl that stank of motor oil, cigarette ash and dog. Recessed into the dash was a dead radio, its cassette-tape slot jammed with calcified gobs of blue tack, cigarette butt-ends and pre-euro-era Irish coins. The dash smelled of fused electricals. Above Arm's head, a row of memorial cards, their laminate covers wilted by age and light, were tucked into the sun visor and a red beaded rosary chain was tangled around the inverted T of the rearview mirror.

Three houses down, two schoolgirls were sitting on a garden wall, talking and smoking. They were in their teens, their figures swollen to shapelessness by puffa jackets and the voluminous skirts of navy-and-green convent plaid heaped up in their laps. It was ten on a Wednesday morning, and the girls, Arm figured, were mitching from school. They were sharing the one cigarette, passing it back and forth and gabbing and rocking their feet from side to side in insistent tandem. Their heads were bent low, they covered their mouths as they spoke, each the other's confidant, and Arm could have happily sat and watched them for the rest of the morning but he sensed movement from Fannigan's house. Dympna was stomping back down the lawn in a way that reminded Arm of his own little boy, Jack. Dympna loomed by the passenger window, made a gun shape with his finger and pointed at Arm's head. Arm popped out his earphones. Dympna's features, which always looked too small for his wide face, were pinched, consternated. His trackie top was zipped right up to his neck, and Arm watched the zipper shiver tautly against the protuberant knot of his Adam's apple. Dympna let out a long sigh, like a mammy.

'Arm, get in there and beat the fuck out of that daft man.'

'What about the mother?'

Dympna held up and opened his left hand. A key adhered to his clammy palm.

'I put her in the bathroom. Fannigan agreed that was best, gave me a hand getting her in there. He's waiting for you in the sitting room.'

'Is he going to make it awkward, you reckon?'

Dympna ran his right hand over the ginger stubble on top of his head, shaved so tight it shone like vapour in the morning light.

'You never know, but I don't think so. He knows it'll go over easier if he just takes it.'

'How easy should it go?' Arm asked.

Dympna smiled wanly, 'Well, don't kill him.'

The story came out last night, when Mary Rose, the third eldest of Dympna's seven sisters, discovered Charlotte— Charlie they all called her—the youngest, weeping hysterically in the upstairs bathroom. Charlie had to be given a cup of warm milk chased by a sedative jigger of whiskey before she calmed down enough to tell what happened.

. 'It's myself I blame,' Dympna had confided on the drive over. 'Letting uncivilised fucking animals like Fannigan past my front door.'

Dympna Devers was twenty-five, a year older than Arm. Dympna sold marijuana, fat green ziplocked bags of the stuff, all over town. The town was small, and Dympna held a monopoly on such business. Fannigan was the eldest of the crew of five dealers currently in Dympna's employ. Fannigan sold out of the industrial estate, where he worked evenings as a production-line stiff in the Allgen medical prosthetics plant.

The Friday evening gone, as he periodically did, Dympna had invited over the crew, Fannigan included, for drinks at the Devers's family home, where his mother June and three of his seven sisters still lived. The Devers were a sociable breed, and liked crowding the house up. The parties tended to putter amicably on into the early hours, and attendees were encouraged to crash on the couch or floor if they had drank, snorted or smoked away the wherewithal to get home in one piece. The problem was that on that last night, Fannigan, completely pig-eyed, had at some point found his way up to young Charlie's bedroom, let himself in, and attempted to stick several parts of himself in under her bedcovers. Charlie had only turned fourteen a couple of weeks ago.

Dympna told Arm all this on the way over. Arm was amazed that Dympna had put the lock on his initial impulses, had waited out the night before taking action; amazed again that Dympna had gone in there and given Fannigan an opportunity to explain himself instead of just caving the man's skull in.

'So did he offer another side, then?' Arm said.

Dympna rolled his little eyes.

'First he claimed he couldn't remember a thing at all. Then he started swearing blind that in the state he was in he thought Charlie was Lisa.'

Lisa was Dympna's second oldest sister, twenty-four, by general consensus the prettiest of the Devers girls; that Fannigan's molestations were intended for another of Dympna's siblings, albeit one of legal age, would have done little to mollify the big man.

'Jesus,' Arm said, 'fair play.'

'No,' Dympna said, 'no fair play at all.'

82

Arm wound the wires of his iPod neatly about the device and placed it on the dash. When he stepped out of the car, Dympna handed him the bathroom key.

'Light damage,' Dympna said, 'lesson damage.'

Fannigan was on the couch in the sitting room, in front of a low wooden coffee table. A shining black plasma hung on the wall, a talk show on, switched to mute. It was a Yank show; tanned people with bleached teeth and sports jackets mooing and grimacing at each other like pantomimes. Arm could hear a clock, an old-fashioned mechanical tick-tocker in the hall, and faint scrabbling noises from behind the bathroom door.

'I don't want to keep her too long in there,' Fannigan said, nodding towards the hall. He was a bit drained-looking, but there was no tremor in his voice. His limbs were pinned to the couch. Fannigan was somewhere in his fifties. He was gaunt, with dirty silver-tinged rocker hair. He wore a bushy grey moustache he presumably considered distinguished, the whited ends tamed into tapered points by regular, finger-tipped applications of spittle, and he might once have been a handsome man. All Fannigan had on were jeans and a vest. His ropey arms were decorated with the murky green-blue blotches of old tattoos, their original shapes and lines mottled into illegibility by age. The lack of clothing was on purpose, Arm decided. Fannigan wanted to advertise the frailty of his scrawny frame.

'Have a seat,' Fannigan said.

Arm stepped forward.

'Arm—' Fannigan said and raised an open hand.

Arm grabbed the back of Fannigan's head and flipped him off the couch onto the floor. Fannigan's cheek smacked the coffee table. He moaned, and a dark rivulet, meaty and viscous, slipped from his mouth. Arm stepped back and guided his foot up under the old man's ribs.

'Up,' Arm said, 'look, Fannigan. Look.'

Fannigan raised his face as requested. Arm hit him two, three, four times. To his credit, Fannigan was still conscious after that, though swimming on his elbows on the carpet. It was often hard to tell if a person was crying in that state—there was usually a lot of liquid running from their face, necessitating all manner of soggy expulsions and clogged snorkelling noises. But Arm thought Fannigan was crying. Certainly, Fannigan was struggling to say something.

'I—I—I didnnnn efffin ged, ged haa nnnnnnickers off!'

Arm hit Fannigan again. There was the wishbone snap of his nose breaking and the old man was clean out. Arm wrenched the plasma from the wall and tucked it under his arm. In the hall, he dropped the key and toed it under the bathroom door. Arm could hear Fannigan's mother scuffling on the other side, groaning, 'Where's my Billy, where's my Billy?'

Arm became friends with Dympna at fifteen. They were in the same school, but hung in different groups and it was not until Dympna showed up at Saint Ignatius Athletic, the local boxing club, that Arm got to know him. Dympna was a porky, eager boy back then, keen to transmute his flab to muscle and learn how to throw a punch. Boxing was Arm's thing; at underage level he had fought his way to county, and briefly, provincial, distinction. Arm had the clear head and cold-bloodedness required by the ring, the knack of detachment. Arm could be buried in the moment of a fight, spun and dizzy and snorting sputum, his body bright and ringing, and yet at the same time occupy a little bubble of lucidity above it all. His punches travelled with just the right weight and restraint, and they had a bounce to them when they landed, the way raindrops splash. And Arm was relentless. If the ref did not intercede, he could pound equably away on a lad until his head fell off.

Because Arm was the best around, Dympna pestered after him to spar. Dympna was barely in shape, and had mediocre form, and both boys knew rightly that Arm would destroy Dympna, but Dympna insisted. After each session they would sit in the bleachers, Dympna staunching a pumping nostril with a wad of cotton or pressing an ice pack to a blown-up eye socket, and at his behest the two would go forensically back over whatever combination of moves Arm had used to demolish him that day. Dympna viewed the beatings as instructional in nature, a mapping out, bruise by bruise, of the vulnerable regions of the body. Arm intuited that even at sixteen Dympna had plans, and that Dympna would need to understand the dynamics of pain, its infliction and its absorption, in order to effect those plans. What Dympna couldn't give a fuck for were the organised formalities and quaint codes of conduct that governed in-the-ring competition, and after he secured what he wanted—Arm, Arm's friendship—he persuaded Arm that he shouldn't either.

Dympna and Arm started smoking dope, lots and lots of dope, and Dympna, who had a connection through the uncles, started selling it. Arm lost his virginity to Lisa and additionally got his dick into Fatima and Christina, the twins. Dympna, who always deferred to the coven wisdom of his sisters, took their plural interest in Arm as a sign of clinching approbation, and brought Arm in permanently as his muscle. Arm's name was Douglas Armstrong, but every creature around knew him as Arm ever since Dympna christened him such. Arm was what Dympna threatened to sic on you if you dared cross him. *Don't make me put the Arm on you*, Dympna would say, though most of the time Arm was required to do little more than hover stone-faced behind Dympna's right shoulder.

On the drive back to the Devers's house Arm kept the window down. He looked in the wing mirror, imagining the ruination he'd dosed upon Fannigan's face dosed on his own. Arm had been beaten badly a couple of times in the ring, of course—had to have ripped eyelids sewn up, the flopping cartilage of a disjointed nose wedged back into place—but nothing too serious, and in Dympna's employ he had suffered little more than an occasional scratch.

Arm watched the Devers's home appear. They lived in a big red-brick, two-storey house on the edge of Farrow Hill estate. The family was of traveller extraction, and though they'd been settled going back three generations, such origins, however distant, were enough for the house to be known locally as The Tinker Mansion, though no one called it that to Dympna's face.

Dympna's cousin Brandon was outside. Brandon was a slope-shouldered, paunchy lad in his twenties, with a round pale face and a shock of long, prematurely white hair that came right down to his arse. He seemed to wear only black T-shirts emblazoned with the name and artwork of various metal bands, and was himself a guitarist in a local band called Satan On Sabbatical. He was standing in the front lawn, his head bent forward, drawing a comb through his hair with girlish solicitude.

Brandon was originally from Guernsey. He'd become involved in some vague, not very serious trouble (vandalism, petty theft, a painted cow) after leaving school and his mother—Dympna's aunt, an obese diabetic divested fairly recently of the toes on one foot—had sent the lad here, ostensibly to spend the summer. That had been a year ago. He was a docile lad, his only passion the pursuit of metal. White wisps of hair floated in the air around him.

Arm hefted the plasma from the backseat.

'How do, Brandon,' Dympna said, and Arm nodded at him.

'Hi,' Brandon said in his soft voice, 'you lads coming to our gig tomorrow?' Satan On Sabbatical was playing in Quillinan's pub on the main street.

'Sure,' Dympna said, 'we'll be right up front with our tits hanging out.'

'He know about what happened to Charlie?' Arm asked Dympna as they went inside.

Dympna shook his head. 'He knows she's been poorly, that's it. No sense sharing the gory details with him.'

They went through the hall, into the sitting room. Lisa and Charlie were on the sofa, watching TV. Charlie was in a bathrobe, her shins, thin as twigs, protruding from the bathrobe's folds into pink-striped socks. She looked lamentably like what she was, a child, and Arm felt good for the throbs in the joints of his fingers.

Lisa was barefoot in shorts of battered denim, with one leg curled up under her, propped on a cushion. She was wearing fake gold earrings, her dark, streak-shot hair piled in a sloppy bun that listed enticingly. She was one of those women who were at their most physically eloquent in a state of casual dishevelment, though as always she had a thick layer of makeup applied to her face; hot pink lipstick, dusky orange foundation trowelled on and eyeliner as vividly black as cinders, and dense, as if each lash was magnified in bold type.

'There's the men,' she said. Arm watched Dympna come round the back of the sofa, put a hand on Charlie's shoulder and nuzzle the top of her head with his nose.

'Grrrrrr,' he said.

'Get off!' Charlie said.

Dympna looked up at Arm.

'Do you not want that?' he said, meaning the plasma. Wiring trailed from the back.

Arm shrugged.

'I thought Charlie might like it.'

'Well aren't you the thoughtful one, Douglas,' Lisa said.

'Say thanks,' Dympna said.

'Thanks,' Charlie said.

June Devers, the mammy, was in the kitchen. She had the breakfast cooked and waiting—sausages and eggs, tomato, soda bread and milky tea. June was a short, broad woman with a wide, freckle-ridden bosom. Her late husband's name, *Neddy*, was tattooed in slender cursive on the inner slope of her left tit. She had the same ruddy face and dinkiness of feature as Dympna, and small, very yellow teeth. She kissed Arm on each cheek, and, as he and Dympna attacked the steaming grub, she asked Arm how his little lad Jack was.

'You know,' Arm said, 'still ticking along in his own world.'

'Such a gorgeous creature,' June said. 'You and that Dory girl, good genes.'

When Arm said he had to leave, Dympna looked up from his plate, 'We'll be talking soon, Arm.'

'He has you at his beck and call,' June said indulgently. On the way out she grabbed Arm's wrist. She slipped two fifties into his hand.

'Thanks for all this, Douglas. Buy some flowers for your girl.'

The girl, who was no longer Arm's girl, Ursula Dory, lived with Arm's son in her parents' house in the Drummond Rise estate, up the other end of town. Arm booted it on foot out the main road. Traffic was sparse but steady; the whoosh of a mammy hatchback or transit van trundling in off the state road sounded like lazy waves breaking on a shore just out of sight.

When Arm got there Ursula was ironing and Jack was up on the kitchen table. Jack was in a T-shirt and nappy, his toes hooked tightly around the table's ledge, like talons. He was gouging apart a slice of bread with his fingers. The position looked precarious, but Jack was a practised indoor climber and percher.

'Well, shameen,' Arm said.

Jack fluted his lips, made a subdued hooting noise, and went back to working on his bread. Jack ate fitfully, with a lot of incidental wastage. He tore off a piece of the bread, put it in his gob, and worked it about until it was a tight wee wad. Sometimes he swallowed, and sometimes he took the wad out and flicked it onto the lino, as he did now. There were half a dozen such wads already littering the floor.

'Stop that,' Ursula said.

Arm snapped two fifties from his snakeskin, added the two June gave him. He folded the notes into a tight tube and waved the tube in front of Jack.

'Hey, Jack, here you go, go buy your mammy something nice,' Arm said, and put the money in his son's hand. Jack was about to put the notes in his mouth when Ursula snatched them away.

'Thanks,' she said unenthusiastically. She pocketed the money and went back to the laundry. The unfolded pile gave off a damp heat, pinkening her whey complexion. There was a fat textbook on the table beside the iron. Ursula was taking evening classes in the community college.

Jack was five. Arm had put the boy in Ursula's belly when she was just gone eighteen, and Jack and Ursula had lived here, with Ursula's ma and da, since he was born. Arm came round perhaps less than he should, but he found it wearying to be in a place where he would only ever be tolerated. Ursula's folks, entirely reasonably, Arm thought, hated him. They hated what he and Ursula's recklessness had thwarted, though they were helpless to do anything other than love the little boy.

'How's he sleeping?' Arm asked.

'Well enough, these days,' Ursula said.

'Will we go to the park, monkey-bar boy?' Arm chucked Jack under the chin.

Arm liked to get the kid out of Ursula's hair, though she was wary of him taking Jack anywhere unfamiliar. Anything other than the usual routine unnerved Jack; new people and places had to be introduced to him in slow stages, or he'd shy, or worse. The boy was in the main docile but capable of ferocious turns, instantaneous eruptions. It had taken several attempts but Arm had got him down to the playground out by the new road, and Jack loved it there now, as long as there were no other kids around. Jack loved to climb and loved the blue-painted jungle gym they'd thrown up. He liked the back-and-forth tacking of the swings and the looping simplicity of the slide; up the steps, down the dented tin chute, repeat, repeat.

'If you can get him into his trousers, sure,' Ursula said.

Jack preferred to go bare-legged, and if left to his own devices would shed any trousers and footwear as soon as possible. Arm shrugged. 'Sure I'll take him like this. Don't think Jack'll be bothered.'

'You will not!' Ursula said and smiled. She had the same sandy blonde hair and blue eyes as Jack, and her face ignited when you could coax a smile onto it, which had never been easy. Ursula was smart, and Arm wondered if he wasn't still in love with her half the time, but she was a wincy, moribund bitch when she wanted to be.

'Serious. I'll take mine off too. Solidarity.'

Jack stuck out his tongue and blew a raspberry, and added a garbled yip as a period. It was clear to Arm that the doctors hadn't a notion about Jack, or his prospects, and were taking the long route in admitting as much. Before Jack was two he had actually picked up a few baby words, but they went away again soon after, like toys he had tired of and abandoned. Jack had talked, and now did not, and the doctors could not tell if he would ever get back to talking again, or when that day might come.

But still, Jack had his noises, and Arm could read the colour and shape of his moods in those noises as plain as day. There were the moos and coos of contentment, the squawks and trills of delight, the stream of burbles that attended his absorption in some odd task, the injurious kitten mewling for when things weren't going his way, and then there was the deep, guttural screaming that stood for itself and nothing else. His tantrums were infrequent, but came on abruptly, and often without identifiable cause. He could become violent, usually to himself, knocking his head against a wall, trying to kick through glass frames or wooden doors, mauling his own fingers until they bled. Anyone who got in his way was fair game for a savage swick. The violence was an undirected venting of pressure, and meant nothing beyond the compulsion of its expression—so hazarded the doctors. It was what it was, like the weather. Intervention was risky, but still, Ursula, tiny-framed and stick-armed herself, would put on oven gloves and tackle the boy every time. Arm told her not to, to let her oul fella grab Jack if anyone was going to, but she kept doing it. She would get him into a bear hug on the couch or floor and hold tight and wait for the rage to drain away.

But today Jack was happy, burbly and sweet-eyed. Arm chucked him under the chin again and Jack playfully snapped his teeth.

'He's going to see the horses later,' Ursula said. 'So don't be gone too long.'

The horses were therapy, recommended by the county hospital shrink. There was a small public-access farm in town that received a state grant in exchange for letting the very young, the very old, and the mentally and physically infirm bother the animals. Jack was scared of creatures smaller and quicker and noisier than him—cats and toddlers disconcerted him, dogs outright terrified him—but he liked the horses. He had gone three or four times now, and on the last visit had consented to be mounted on one of the smaller beasts and trotted gently around a paddy, and had remained calm and composed the entire time, according to Ursula.

'Tiger cub, hup, hup. You're a strange kid,' Arm said, and could feel Ursula watching, listening. 'You're a strange kid and getting stranger.'

In his runners Jack was a stomper. All his shoes were runners, all had Velcro straps, laces were an unnecessary complication. As he and Arm headed to the park he smashed the pavement with the flats of his soles like he was stomping on cardboard boxes. It seemed to give him immense satisfaction.

Ursula had helped Arm get Jack into his Spider-Man jacket—the cuffs, like the cuffs of all Jack's jackets, mutilated and raggy with chew marks—and trackie bottoms, and then the pair had set out. Jack knew exactly where they were going, and Arm was proud of the ease with which his son discerned the route, though even a dog could learn to do that.

The park was empty. Jack tore across the tarmac, leapt up onto the jungle gym, and zigzagged his way to its summit, negotiating the levels with hurling simian dexterity. Up top, he hooted triumphantly and bent his head and started tonguing the blue metal bars, lustily French kissing the things.

'Stop that!' Arm said.

Jack registered the sharpness in Arm's tone and looked up. He wiped his mouth with the back of his hand and appeared almost guilty for a moment. Arm sunk onto the bench and waved at his boy, *sorry*. Instantly Jack appeared content again, and began to low and bark happily to himself. The sky behind Jack wasn't any colour at all really, just banded with watery shade lower to the horizon, where distant weather was stirring.

'Hector was awful itchy on the phone. Short and itchy,' Dympna said.

Friday afternoon. The sun had been shining and the rain had been falling all morning. Dympna and Arm were heading uptown in the shitbox, and Dympna, driving, was talking in a low voice out of the side of his mouth. Dympna, Arm knew, tended to go tight-jawed when apprehensive.

'What about?' Arm asked, though he could guess.

Dympna glanced at Arm. He squinched his lips and emitted a rhetorical tut.

'How'd they find out?' Arm asked.

'The mammy, I reckon. Chief disseminator of all information in this world and the next.'

'She seemed fine about it the other day.'

'I thought so.'

'You think they're going to want something done?' Arm asked.

'Something, alright.'

Hector and Paudi Devers were the younger brothers of Dympna's deceased father. They lived ten miles outside of town, on a secluded farm at the end of a barely navigable dirt track in the bogged and heathered foothills of the Nephin Mountains, and where, in conjunction with their regular farmerly duties, they cultivated an especially fragrant and potent strain of marijuana. They grew the plant hydroponically, in the permanent twilight of a temperature-controlled, UV-lit nursery built into the storage basement of a cattle shed. The operation was small but professionally appointed in scale, and the uncles produced enough weed to enable Dympna to service the appetite of every burned-out factory worker and delinquent schoolkid within the town limits. Arm was cool to them. The uncles were necessary to Dympna's operation, but they were mercurial birds, easy to spook. Arm knew of at least two occasions inside the last couple of years where they had abruptly claimed they were going to give up growing, and Dympna had to beg and plead with them, and each time offer a bigger cut, to change their minds.

Arm and Dympna dropped out once a month to load up on a fresh supply and pay the uncles what they were owed. He and Dympna were, as far as Arm knew, the uncles' only regular visitors.

Hector and Paudi kept the farm locked down, a hold-out against the world. They had an in-house armoury stocked with several hand guns, a pair of shotguns, and a semiautomatic hunting rifle with a mounted telescopic sight. They had flak jackets and camo gear, and both men were adept at improvising small explosive devices from basic domestic and farming ingredients, or so they claimed. They had shown Dympna and Arm something called a siege cupboard, where they kept an eighteen-month supply of tinned soup and dry goods. They owned two hulking Alsatians trained to lock jaws around the jugulars of grown men on command. The basement in which they grew the weed was extensively rigged and booby trapped, to be razed at short notice in the worst-case scenario.

They rarely left the premises, and certainly never at the same time. Dympna and Arm's trips out to them were short. Arm preferred to stay in the car while Dympna went inside to parley and complete the necessary exchanges.

Dympna and Arm were scheduled in fact to head to the farm the next day, and so would not have expected to hear from either of the uncles until then. But Hector had rung Dympna this morning, out of the blue, requesting a meet in Lally's pool arcade on the main street, at two.

*   *   *

Lally's was dim and cool, its gloomy space filled with six full-size pool tables. There were a couple of games in session, the players' low talk lost beneath the overlapping reports of the balls colliding across each bright rectangle of baize, and now and then the prompt gurgle of a ball rattlingly sunk. The windows had fine mesh grilles over them, a penitentiary detail no regular much seemed to mind. There was no drinking licence for the premises, but the enterprising Mark Scriney sold cans and bottles out of a portable ice box at twice their supermarket prices. No woman had crossed Lally's threshold in years, if ever.

Hector was in the back, sat at one of the flimsy chipboard tables arranged along the wall. An elderly man was with him, talking volubly while Hector only listened.

Dympna's uncle was a squat, sturdy man in his fifties, with a paunch, wide forearms and a face rendered cracked and red from decades of working in the elements. He was spruced and prinked for his afternoon in civilisation, dressed in a cuff-linked white shirt and navy pullover. His black hair, as yet only negligibly tipped with silver, was boxily trimmed and waxed. He would be heading to Roscommon later that day, Arm knew. The more presentable and socially adroit of the uncles, Hector had a woman by the name of Mirkin squirrelled away in Ballintober, a widow with whom he'd been pursuing a glacially paced courtship for the last three years; the woman, also in her fifties, had until recently lived with her ninety-something mother and, fretful of scandalising the old crone, had only permitted her suitor to visit one night every few weeks. Though the mother had died a couple of months back, the frequency of Hector and the widow's rendezvous had not, as yet, increased. Hector, though, did not seem to mind, and Arm suspected the bitty, piece-meal nature of the relationship was in fact one of its prime appeals. Dympna had his own theories concerning the courtship. He was convinced that the widow was sitting on a lot of money, a potential double inheritance, and that Hector was on its track, painstakingly working the slow grift.

As Arm and Dympna got closer, Arm copped the smell coming off the second man, the eye-wateringly ripe stench of dried-in adult piss, which explained why Hector was leaning back on the rear legs of his seat. Hector's arms were folded across the shelf of his stomach and the wings of his nose were drawn narrow, a crinkle of supressed disgust edging his smile.

'Ah, these here are the ones I was waiting for,' he said, cutting off the old man, who twisted round in his seat to take in Arm and Dympna.

'Your young fellas?' the man croaked.

'The ginner's the nephew, and his friend used box for the county. Fine stumps of men.'

'They're alright,' the man said without enthusiasm.

'Are we interrupting?' Dympna said.

'Not at all, Mick here was just telling me a fascinating theory he has about Jaysus.'

'Jaysus?' Dympna said.

'Our Lord and Saviour,' the man said.

'His theory,' Hector elaborated when the man did not go on, 'is that Jaysus had a twin. A brother, and when they nailed the first one to the cross and buried him in that cave, his followers robbed the body and had the other lad show up three days later, claiming he was Jaysus come back.'

The old man watched Arm and Dympna as Hector talked. One eye was gummed near shut. He was wearing mud-caked, laceless Reebok runners, no socks, plum tracksuit bottoms shiny with filth, and a mustard sports jacket over a faded WORLD CUP '94 T-shirt. In his hand he clutched a plastic shopping bag with what appeared to be a bunch of other plastic bags folded up inside it.

'Alright,' Dympna said cautiously, 'sounds okay. Sounds a lot more plausible, like, than coming back from the dead.'

'It does,' the man said curtly. He pressed his knuckles into the table and gingerly raised himself from his seat.

'Nice talking to you, always good to meet a man with a cast of a brain in his head, always good.' He turned and the skunky hum of piss turned in the air and departed with him.

'What the fuck was that about?' Dympna said, coughing and clearing his throat and taking the seat the man had vacated. Arm dragged a seat over from the next table along.

'That wretched old boy's harmless,' Hector said. 'His ilk aren't what I'm worried about.'

'And what is the worry now, Heck?' Dympna said.

'Don't be sighing like a man who's already got to the end of what he thinks I'm about to say. This one,' Hector nodded at Arm, 'understands the virtue of keeping his trap shut and letting a man get to the end of his own sentences.'

'You sounded put out on the phone, Heck, that's all,' Dympna said, interlinking his stubby fingers and again clearing his throat.

'I heard—' Hector began, hauling himself upright in his seat, which caused his stomach to well against the lip of the table, 'about this fella. What's his name?'

'Fannigan,' Dympna said.

'Fannigan. What he did to the young one.'

Dympna's tongue skittered between his teeth.

'You heard about what he tried to do. She's okay. We're taking care of it. We have taken care of it, as a matter of fact.'

'Have you now?' Hector said.

'Yes,' Dympna said.

'I care about my family. About my brother's family. Me and Paudi both,' Hector raised an inclusive palm towards Dympna, then put out the other hand, like Paudi was right there, sitting beside him.

Paudi was the scarier seeming of the uncles. He was thin and very tall, with a briar patch of grey-black hair and a torrentially unkempt Taliban beard. He had hard black eyes that put Arm in mind of the taxidermied foxes and stoats his own Uncle Fred kept in glass display cabinets behind the bar of his pub.

'So do I,' Dympna said.

'She's a child,' Hector said, 'a child. What have you done about it?'

Dympna was about to say something but Hector put the hand up. *Stop.*

'It's my business to sort,' Dympna said, looking levelly at his uncle.

'Is it now?' Hector said. The crinkle crept back into his mouth corner.

Dympna shifted in his chair.

'If you can't handle it you should've called us in.'

'It's. Fucking. Handled,' Dympna said.

'Is it now?' A derisive whicker escaped Hector's nose. 'I don't know about that at all, and Paudi doesn't know about that. And your father, God bless him, would never leave it end there, either. Retribution wouldn't have even begun, as far as he'd be concerned.'

Dympna closed his eyes and opened them.

'Believe me,' he said. 'Fannigan won't step out of line in his life ever again.'

Hector was silent for a moment. He plucked at a cuff link, apparently considering Dympna's assertion, then turned his eyes on Arm.

'The muscle,' he said, 'young Armstrong. Tell me, Douglas. If what happened to that child happened to yours, would you leave the matter as is?'

Arm said nothing.

Dympna sighed. 'We can't be attracting attention, Heck. It's dealt with.'

Hector rapped the table with his hand.

'Just be glad, lad, we don't hold you more accountable. Just be glad we consider you a fool rather than a coward.'

Arm could see Dympna was on the verge of going over. Blood flooded the plains of his face. He nipped his bottom lip with his teeth and breathed out hard.

'And so what do you think you're going to do?'

Hector pushed back his chair and stood up. He surveyed the room, and the other patrons made sure they were looking some other way. Satisfied those within earshot were at least feigning obliviousness, Heck smiled sadly and leaned down close.

'What we shouldn't have to, cos it should already be done.'

Arm watched him go. Dympna stared hard at the wall, waiting for his simmer to abate, and Arm knew enough to say nothing.

Arm and Dympna parted ways for the afternoon. Arm took a walk through town and was struck by the notion of seeing Jack with the horses.

The town farm was a walled-off half acre of picture-book pasture tucked between the technical college and the swimming centre. Out front, Arm strolled past an empty whitewashed cottage, its door open, radio on inside, a row of wizened pansies keeled over on the peeling red sill. In back he sidestepped dried animal patties cratered with hoofmarks and followed a trampled track to the gate of a large fenced field.

There were two adults and half a dozen kids, Jack among them, at the far end of the field, all watching a woman on a slim white horse. She was goading the beast into brief gallop bursts, letting it bolt at full steam for a bit before bringing it back down to a jangling trot.

Watching along with Arm was a kid in a wheelchair and an older lad in rubber croc shoes. The older lad, tubby, was eating a fluorescent green candy bar. He was maybe in his twenties, with black framed glasses and a monastic looking, wispy beard circumscribing his blubbery face from lock to lock. He had those black tribal rings in his ears that stretched out the lobes. He was the kid's minder, Arm guessed. The kid had an enormous head and a puny body pinned and bracketed by an elaborate metal frame built down over the wheelchair. A metal halo studded with screws and bolts encircled his skull and kept his oversized head and undersized neck firmly in place; further bolts, straps and supporting spokes attended his arms and legs. The modified wheelchair looked like a cross between a rally-car roll cage and a medieval rack, but Arm supposed it was alleviating the kid's suffering in some way.

The minder caught Arm looking and smiled.

The rider led the way as the group started over towards Arm, the kid and the minder. The narrow barrel of the horse's torso hitched from side to side in a lazy, sultry way. At the gate the horse turned sideways. Up close, Arm could see that its hide was not a uniform white, but a light, chalky grey, speckled with luminous patches of white. It lowered the suede derrick of its tremendous head and neck and began nipping at a spiky patch of grass.

'See the horsey, Terry?' the lad with the stretched lobes said to the caged kid.

The rider was young too, with an aquiline nose, freckles, and black curly hair. She opened her mouth and politely alarmed American came out.

'Can I help you with anything?'

'That's my boy,' Arm said, pointing at the group, 'Jack Dory.'

'Oh Jack,' she said. The kids had caught up, swarming at the gates.

'He loves his horseys,' she said, dismounting.

Jack was looking at the rider out of the side of his face. He was wearing a crooked little grin, as if he were in the midst of some prurient calculation.

'Jack!' Arm shouted.

Jack considered Arm sceptically, fluttered his hands either side of himself, and hopped in place. Then a big drooler, a rock-skulled six-foot manchild with a pudding-bowl haircut and a ratty scrawl of hair on his upper lip dundered by, knocking Jack to the ground. Jack screeched and immediately became interested in something in the grass by his foot. The drooler bent over and commenced groaning into the ear of the horse as he ran his knuckles up and down its neck. The horse, evidently conditioned to such chaos, continued to chomp unperturbed at the grass.

'Hey now, Kevin,' the rider said, grabbing his arm and pushing the avidly molesting manchild gently back.

'He's autistic too,' she said to Arm, bending down to swat away the cigarette butt Jack was about to start eating. She grabbed him by the elbow and dragged him to his feet, which was about the only way to get Jack to his feet. Jack coughed and laughed again. The other carers, two grey-haired women with windburned faces, were frantically corralling the rest of the kids. A girl, no more than ten, in a purple leotard onesie and battered fur-trimmed snow boots, hissed and snarled as one of the women secured her in a delicate arm-lock and frog-marched her out the gate.

'This is some fucking zoo,' Arm said.

'You shouldn't be here,' the rider said to Arm, her smile fading, 'these kids have a schedule.'

'I just came to see the horses,' Arm said.

Satan On Sabbatical was due onstage at nine. Arm got to Quillinan's early, installed himself at the bar, nursed an ice water and lime, and kept an eye on the door traffic until the man himself walked in, Lisa on his arm. Dympna chin-jutted in greeting and checked his stride to cede right of way to a couple of young ones cutting across him. Arm watched him register their behinds and dolefully smack his lips. There was only a certain type of town female that would go with Dympna. Ranged against him were the taint of his tinker lineage and the spectre of his criminality, as well as the persistent low rumours that suggested he fucked his own beautiful sisters, which made the Fannigan business all the more galling, Arm figured; whatever his other flaws, Dympna was a knight to those girls.

They came his way, arm in arm.

'How do,' Arm said.

'Let's get this party started,' Lisa chanted.

Quillinan's was getting full, buzzy. Brandon and his bandmates had been tireless in dredging up interest. The little stage space was way in the back, and Brandon was out there already, sitting on a stool, an unplugged electric guitar resting faceup across his knees. He was scratching out the bare bones of a melody on the dormant instrument. Dympna gave Brandon a thumbs-up and then sculpted his palms in front of his chest, proffering the promised titties. Lisa whooped and clapped her hands above her head. Arm watched the bracelets and bangles adorning her wrists slide from her wrists and bottleneck at her elbows.

'Self-expression,' Dympna muttered.

'Hah?' Arm said.

'I should've learned to play guitar. Who the fuck would need a mouth then?'

'You'd need a mouth to sing,' Arm said.

'Fuck the water, it's time to drink.'

Just after nine, sufficiently wired and amped, the band struck up an introductory instrumental rumble that got a bit of a crowd drifting towards the stage. Brandon stood before the mike bulb, chin fixed to his chest, his fingers writhing along the guitar's fret as the thunderhead of noise roiling around him grew in intensity. He laughed nervously, muttered thanks for coming, and began to scream.

Lisa slipped into the crowd to mingle, and Arm and Dympna hung back at the bar, downing Jack Daniel's and Cokes. Dympna cracked one set of knuckles, then the other.

'Fuck them,' he said finally.

'Who, now?' Arm asked.

'Fuckin' you know who. They want to get involved at this end fine. Get involved. Don't just lecture me because I actually went ahead and dealt with a problem.'

Dympna looked at Arm. 'I dealt with it.'

'I know,' Arm said.

There was a pinch on Arm's arse and Lisa ranged up by his side. She smelled good, she smelled close. She hooked her arm around Arm's neck and asked if there was a single man in here with the wherewithal to show a girl a good time. Arm slanted his eyes at her. She tweaked his cheek.

'Solid but unspectacular, love, that's you.'

'More drinks. Go. Go,' Dympna declaimed sourly, jabbing Arm's shoulder. Arm shed Lisa with a brusque duck and backstep and adjourned to the bar.

The rider from the farm was there. She was flanked by a couple of girls Arm half recognised, town natives in bitty black dresses, sand-blasted with fake tan. The rider was tomboyishly functional by comparison, in high-top sneakers, jeans and a corduroy jacket with elbow patches. The affiliation with the natives seemed cursory. Possibly housemates, Arm speculated, or maybe the two worked with her on the farm in some capacity.

They were all drinking cocktails, red syrup and crushed ice concoctions that resembled slush steeped in blood. The natives were daintily sipping from straws and watching the room to see who was watching them. The rider, elbows on the bar, back to the din, fiddled in a desultory way with her drink, working her straw through its ice-clogged depths. She picked a larger lump of ice from the drink and slipped it in her mouth.

'Well,' Arm said.

She looked at him.

'I was at the horses today,' Arm explained.

'Oh. Yeah. Planning any more unscheduled visits?' she said, biting down on the ice.

'Well, you know,' Arm said, and cleared his throat.

'I don't know, actually. You guys have a way of saying that. You know. Saying nothing.'

'I guess I didn't think there'd be any harm to it.'

'You just have to be careful, working with those kids,' she said.

'No doubt,' Arm said.

'You know, one of them is yours. You know they're delicate.'

'I don't know if delicate is the word. The kid seems to like it there alright, though.'

She fiddled some more with her drink, then scowled over her shoulder.

'What's up with the band. Is it ironic or something?'

'I know them.'

'They're fucking heinous,' she said.

'Well, I guess that's how they're meant to sound.'

'Friends of yours?'

'Yeah,' Arm said.

'But you know everyone, right? Local. How could you not.'

'I don't,' Arm assured her.

'What about that guy?' she said, pointing at Dympna.

'He's a buddy,' Arm admitted.

'I bought some stuff off him before,' she said.

'Hah,' Arm said.

'Shady character,' she said.

Arm flagged down the bartender and ordered a round.

'How'd you end up here?' Arm said.

'Here, here?' she said. She huffed out her cheeks. 'I should get my backstory tattooed to my fucking forehead. It'd save having to recite it every time I open my mouth.'

'You've relatives this way,' Arm ventured.

She scoffed, 'No. No. This is virgin territory for me. I was in Dublin, in college, for a while. Then I applied for and followed down the job. I can stay for like another half a year, if the funding for the farm doesn't get cut and my visa holds out.'

'How's the money?' Arm asked.

'I do it for the love,' she said.

'And what do you do if the money's cut?'

'What will your boy do, is the question I'd ask if I were you,' she said. 'Me. I'll be fine.' She grazed the tip of her nose with a knuckle. There was a puncture dot above one nostril, where a piercing would go. 'The world's a big place and you can go anywhere. And actually'—she caught the barman's eye and made a curt circling motion above her drink—'so could you. You were born and bred right here, am I right? What's a guy in his prime do around here?'

'I'm retired,' Arm said.

'Retired. From what?'

'I used to box.'

'But you don't anymore? You're pretty young for retired.'

'I'm old enough. You've to be hungry and senseless for it.'

'And you're not?'

'There was a lot of conditioning, a routine you couldn't skimp on. I lost my spring.'

'So that's that. You do a thing and you're good at it, presumably, and then one day you . . . just . . . stop.'

Arm took a sip of his drink. 'I keep in trim. I can take down a civilian no worries, but once it goes that spring never really comes back.'

'That's a sad story,' she said.

Arm shrugged.

'You're depressing.'

'Cheers,' Arm said.

'That's okay, though,' she said, and took a drink. Arm stood beside her because there was no reason he shouldn't. And neither did she seek to slink away, and after a moment Arm realised she didn't necessarily want to. He leaned in enough so she'd hear.

'You have to want to hurt people. That's what the spring is. You have to keep wanting to hurt people.'

Arm could see their faces in the bar mirror, looming like moons above the miniature skyline of spirit bottles arranged along the back shelf. The neon changed colour and the light caught her nose, and this time Arm noticed the way it was set, and it had been set, just barely imperfectly. It looked like an old break and Arm was about to ask what happened, but right then Dympna clamped him on the shoulder.

His measly eyes were red-rimmed and his cheeks puce. Ignoring the girl, he wheeled Arm away from the light of the bar and into a corner.

'Douglas, tell me now. Can we trust them?'

Arm looked over his shoulder. The rider was talking to the girls. She said something and popped her eyebrows, prompting a giggle from the natives.

'Hector, Paudi,' Dympna said.

'They supply,' Arm said, 'if we don't have them we don't have nothing.'

'They won't let this Fannigan thing drop.'

'You think they'll carry through on it?' Arm said.

'I think they will. I think they'll lift him from the street and take him out there and feed him to their dogs. I think they don't give a fuck about anything after that, the shit storm that'll follow. They don't believe in the guards, jail, not really. Fuck, they barely believe in this town. They live out in the fucking wilds with the stones and the dogs and their guns and they think that's all there really is.'

Arm looked to the bar, but the girls were drifting away through the crowd. The rider did not look back, but there was something in her carriage, in the alignment of her neck and shoulder blades, that suggested she knew she was being watched go.

The night went on. The band churned out an hour of stuff to increasing indifference and relieved cheering when they finished and the DJ took over. The young ones flocked to the floor. Arm watched them, a tribe of women stamping and twisting, and he wondered; where are all the fellas?

'Good night anyway,' Dympna said, 'and fuck the rest of it.'

Dympna's eyes were wobbling in their sockets. Arm felt nicely dented too. Arm patted Dympna's shoulder and stepped out onto the dance floor. Spumes of dry ice rolled between the commingling bodies. Arm turned and knew she'd be there. The rider, bobbing in place behind her two mates, both of whom were wrapped round fellas. She smiled at him, flicked the brows in a way Arm figured for consent. Arm smiled and leaned in. Got a taste of the lips before she drew back and her hand was up on his throat.

'What the fuck,' she mouthed at him over the music. Arm shrugged and hung his head at a contrite angle, then stooped in again. She took another step back and at least smiled ruefully this time. 'Nooo,' she mouthed, and shook her head like Arm was an idiot.

Arm pointed to the smoking area, meaning let's go talk, then.

'Not tonight,' she shouted, grinning again and giving him a pitying squeeze on the arm before stepping off.

Arm watched her go. He thought, that's another story.

Arm left Quillinan's near two, and figured a walk would help wick away the worst of the hangover that was bearing down on his tomorrow. He started for the outskirts of town, out along the quay road. The road stuck more or less parallel to the path that the Mule River cut towards the coast a couple of miles farther on. Arm's intention was to get as far as the strand a mile out then loop back around, a nice three-quarter hour jaunt. Arm had his music in as he walked. After a while he saw a body ahead of him. Arm slowed his tread, recognising the sedimentary rinse of silver through the hair, the scarecrow elbows and bandy-legged lope. Fannigan, like Arm, was taking the scenic route home from whatever establishment he'd elected to get hammered in.

Arm popped out the headphones and stowed the buds inside his jacket, where they continued to palpitate against his chest. Eyes on the back of Fannigan's head, he sped up, taking care to dampen his footfall. Fannigan was oblivious as Arm glided right into step beside him.

'Well, soldier,' Arm said.

Fannigan jumped, his entire frame bouncing like a rubber band. He stifled a cry and swung his gaze towards the river, twenty feet below. After a moment, his eyes dragged themselves back around to Arm, as they had to.

'Jesus, Douglas lad, how are you?' Fannigan croaked with as much composure as he could muster. He had matching black eyes, the sockets pulped and swollen, a band of ragged cotton dressing tacked over his nose.

Arm threw an arm across Fannigan's shoulders and steered him into the riverside wall. Fannigan mumbled, 'What—' right as Arm flipped him. He went headfirst, spinning, sliding over mud, grass and stones. Arm looked both ways—no body or car in eyeshot—and hopped the wall. Quickly he slipped his sneakers from his feet and jammed them beneath a rock. Fannigan just lay there and watched, marsupial eyes blinking out of the dark; it did not occur to him to pick himself up and scramble, to try to run away.

'Up,' Arm said.

Arm could practically hear the laggard cranking of the sot's brain as it tried to process what was happening. Obediently Fannigan got to his feet and began to pat himself down, which only succeeded in dabbling the wet muck farther across his clothes. He was wearing a black Celtic rainjacket with luminous green trim, a sweatshirt, jeans and buckled boots.

'What's happening?'

'Move,' Arm said.

'What?' Fannigan said.

Arm rapped him on the forehead like knocking on a door and repeated his request.

'Turn. Downstream.' Arm jabbed Fannigan between his shoulder blades until he commenced moving. 'The uncles got wind. I hope you knew they always would.'

Arm watched Fannigan's shoulders go rigid then slacken. Fannigan shook his head, glanced back at Arm.

'You are not them,' he said.

'What?'

Fannigan's whiskers twitched.

'You are not them.'

'Keep going,' Arm said.

They walked, Arm following Fannigan in silence, until he decided they were far enough along. He put his hand on Fannigan's shoulder. The Mule was at its widest point here, maybe fifty feet across, and the noise of the current had become industrially loud.

'Jacket,' Arm shouted. Fannigan turned around, took it off and handed it over. Arm balled it and threw it onto the water. It hit the surface and in an instant was snatched away, shedding a curl of froth as it was ferried along for a few moments before sinking into the black.

'Take off the boots, the rest of your clothes.'

'What?'

He was beginning to get a grasp of the situation. Arm had invoked the uncles; Fannigan knew what that meant. The uncles, Dympna was right, Arm knew, they'd butcher Fannigan. They'd use him for sport, and take their time doing so. They'd feed his bones to their curs, and sooner or later decide that Dympna's show of leniency had demonstrated a dangerous weakness at this end of the operation.

Fannigan took his time undressing. The boots he worked off first, then he drew up and off the sweatshirt and the vest beneath.

'Leave them there,' Arm said, toeing a spot in the dirt. Fannigan dropped the shirt and vest, and was soon shivering in a way Arm found hard to watch. Fannigan's torso was pale as milk, his chest hair a scutty fuzz petering down to his navel. His tattoos, in the dark, looked like bruises on his arms.

'Dympna . . .' he said, 'Dympna said this,' he touched his bandaged face, 'Dympna said this was the end of it.'

'Trousers, c'mon,' Arm said.

'Is this happening?' Fannigan said as he stepped out of his pants. 'Oh Christ, I'm naked,' he muttered, 'I'm in the fucking nip.'

Fannigan began to fold his trousers, lining up the legs, then halving and halving them again, until it was a neat, bundled parcel of denim. This small civilised feat accomplished, he began to shake his head.

'No, No, No. This joke's over. I'm not putting up with this. Fuck this!' Fannigan motioned to move past Arm but it was a cursory effort. Arm rested the heel of his hand on Fannigan's collarbone.

'Nearly, it's over,' Arm assured him.

'Christ, can I have a smoke then?'

'In a minute,' Arm said.

'There's no time!' Fannigan said. He had the blinky, nervous energy of a dreamer jilted suddenly awake. Fannigan looked urgently left and right, then up into the sky, at the scratchy stars and that cute old sphinx-faced cunt of a moon, up there watching and still keeping schtum after all these years. He let out another growl, a scouring phlegm-clearer, boggy and granulated and liquidly rich. He hocked and spat at Arm's feet.

'What time is it?' he said.

'Must be three,' Arm said.

'That's right, that's right,' Fannigan said, wiping his mouth with his forearm. 'You feeling okay?' he said to Arm.

'I am,' Arm said.

Arm hunkered down where Fannigan had spat and dragged the boots over and piled the shirt and jumper on top of them. Fannigan, standing, still had his jocks and socks on. The socks were a particularly sad affair, Arm noted; once white, they were grimed to grey, cheap and nubbled and flecked with holes. Arm looked up at Fannigan.

'Put the trousers down here with the rest,' Arm said.

Fannigan was upright and had the upright's advantage of height. A part of Arm wanted to scream at him to take his chance. To push Arm over, or run, or smash Arm's skull with whatever conviction he could channel into his fists; just to try. But the acquiescent fucker only did as he was told, crouching down to Arm's level and placing the folded jeans on top of the other clothes.

'Douglas,' he said. It was dark, but Arm could feel Fannigan's eyes on him. Fannigan had been tuning in and out of this scenario, but he was back now, emphatically here, a lucid and crawlingly beseeching note in Arm's name as he mouthed it. A plea.

'Douglas,' he said it again. 'Listen. Listen. When I was a boy—'

It was right there, half sunk in the mud. Arm snugged his hand around it, a smooth, weighty oval, and aimed for Fannigan's temple, where a delta of veinwork tremulously pulsed. The rock crushed into his head with a flat thud. His eyelids fluttered and he flopped bonelessly down onto the grass.

Arm had his arms in under Fannigan's frame as quick as he could manage, and hefted the man up. Fannigan's body was warm, and felt as if it might be convulsing a little. Arm waded into the river, moving deeper and deeper until the cold was cutting across the tops of his thighs, through his jeans. Arm puffed out his chest and threw Fannigan out towards the middle. He hit the water, sent up a plume of spray and was promptly spooled away on the current.

Arm clambered back up onto the bank and watched him go. Facedown and arse up, Fannigan's body was periodically sucked under the surface before bobbing into sight again. Soon it was nothing more than a diminishing speck in the narrowing turbulence, and then it was gone, baywards to the open sea.

Arm considered the wilted totem of clothing piled by the water's edge. He figured these leavings would make it appear all the more premeditated, would tell the story of how Fannigan, in a suicidal funk, had ritualistically shed his shitty gear before throwing himself in the Mule. Arm picked up the rock he'd hit Fannigan with and pocketed it. He told himself that the dent on

Fannigan's head would be explained as him dashing against rocks as he was carried to sea. He was a drunk and a waster, Fannigan, and save for his mother Arm didn't think anyone, neither the guards nor the coroner nor any other soul, would look to pursue an explanation beyond the apparent when it came to piecing together the why of his end.

Arm clambered back up towards the road, stepping on stones where he could, smooshing the impressions his feet had left in the softer ground on the way down, leaving Fannigan's bootprints intact. He squeezed his runners back on and inched his nose out over the wall's lip; no traffic or souls about. He slipped over. His iPod was still going in his jacket. There were thorn ends and snarls of sap-coated twigs stuck to his clothes. He batted down the shoulders and sleeves of his jacket.

Arm plugged in the buds, slipped his hood up, and resumed walking right out of town. His trousers, wringing, dried as he went. Eventually he found himself following the familiar wrought-iron railings that looked out over the strand. The railings were eaten through, thinned to crusted spindles of rust at their most exposed points. Beyond them lay the rush-topped hillocks and sandbars, the sand milk-blue in the moonlight. Arm scanned the boiling surf for a long time, watched the way each wave rose, evolved like a fortification, and then collapsed.

It was nearing four in the morning as Arm headed back into town. A couple of teenage lads were coming the opposite way, on the other side of the road. Arm took out his earphones and listened as one vociferated to the other about almost bating the head off a third lad back in the pub or club or wherever they'd been, the boaster milling his fists around, clumsily shadow-boxing the air and his cohort cackling along. They were oblivious to Arm. He was on the riverside of the road, and could hear the Mule, and couldn't help but listen out for a voice or scream or roar, because even though Arm knew the man was almost certainly already dead he was still susceptible to the dreamlike dread that Fannigan had somehow eluded the laws of the perishable world and staged a resurrection.

But *Ssshhhhhhhhhhh* went the water.

And *Haaahhhhhhhhhhhhhh* went the wind.

And from off in the nearing distance of the town centre came the calm hum of the taxis as they made their appointed circuits through what was left of the night.

Arm's folks had him late, and only him. A single-child family was a rarity around here, where households teemed with ever-expanding factions of brothers and sisters. Arm's mother was a schoolteacher, forty-two at the time of his birth. His da was already fifty. The da ran a delivery truck out of the local bun factory along the western seaboard for thirty-two years straight and when he walked through the door in the evenings he trailed in his wake a fragrance of cinnamon and currants. His parents' hair was grey by the time Arm started primary school, and though they raised him right and raised him well, Arm sometimes wondered if he wasn't just a late concession to the perennial babymaking thriving away about them. Good old Maye and Trevor Armstrong. Arm and they had always got on and maybe too much. Too much civility, too much mellowness; though it was clear to them that there was an aspect to the run of his life Arm kept from them, they refrained from prying. They doted on Jack, and doted on the idea of Ursula; they chided Arm for not sticking with a girl that lovely.

They saw Arm with Dympna and said nothing at all.

It was their only real fault, this enduring inability to ever think the worst of their son.

When Arm came to the next morning he could hear them downstairs in the kitchen, making breakfast. The noise of their domestic routine got Arm to dwelling on Fannigan's mother, old and frail and alone in this world for good now, though she did not yet know it. He pulled a naggin of Jameson's from the foot of his bed and took a few scouring hits, looking to snap himself out of such useless, malign sentiments.

Arm showered, put on a white vest, his good denim shirt, and made his way down to the Dorys. The low sky was slabbed with rifts of cloud the colour and texture of raw animal fat. Ursula's mother was out front, unloading groceries from the backseat of the family Vauxhall.

'Can I help?' Arm asked, hovering at the foot of the driveway with his hands in his pockets. He had the stone flecked with Fannigan's blood with him. He had not yet decided where or how best to dispose of it, and figured in the interim he should keep it close.

Margaret Dory regarded Arm. She had a narrow, taut face and pale blue eyes that made no bones about boring right through him.

'Douglas. Urs and Jack aren't here. No, I'm fine,' she said.

'Where they gone?'

'Over to the town farm.'

'Guess I'll drop down so. You think that'd be alright?'

Margaret considered Arm's question. He could see she was thrown by his requesting permission.

'Well, Douglas, well I'm sure it'd be okay.'

Arm pulled his hand from the weighted pocket and offered a brisk polite wave. Margaret Dory looked at Arm like he wasn't there.

The cottage was abandoned. The noise of the radio drifted from inside, and the browned flower-husks on the sill shivered dryly in the breeze. Fresh deposits of shit stubbled the trampled track to the main field. Ursula and Jack were by the gate, their backs to Arm. Jack was in his Spider-Man jacket, standing on the bottom rung of the three-beam fence and baying elatedly as the horse and rider completed a stately lap of the field. Arm came up quietly behind him and grabbed at his shoulders, but Jack didn't so much as flinch. It was as if he was expecting Arm's touch at exactly that moment, and perhaps he was. The kid was a mystery from every angle of approach.

Arm chucked him on the cheek, very lightly, attempted the same on Ursula. She slapped at his hand and scowled.

'No offense meant,' he said.

'What are you doing here?' she said.

'Your mam told me where you were.'

The rider and her horse were coming over. The rider stepped down from the saddle and approached the fence.

'Hiiiiii Jack,' she said, and turned to Arm, 'the boxer.'

'How do.'

'Hi,' she said to Ursula. 'You're Jack's mom?'

'Yes,' Ursula said.

'Rebecca. I'm the horse lady.'

'And you've met Douglas here?'

'Douglas? Yeah, he's been here before. He's been around.'

Ursula looked at Arm.

'I'm taking an interest,' he said.

Jack was reaching towards the horse, outstretched fingers writhing in acquisitive agony, as if the animal was a toy he could pick up. The horse turned to the open field. It twitched an ear and considered the middle distance; clouds in boil about the peak of Nephin. The uncles' farm was situated in a cloistered ruck of lowland not far from the foot of the mountain, and when he squinched his eyes Arm was convinced he could make out the buildings from here.

'You want a go, Douglas?' Rebecca asked.

'Ah, I'm alright.'

'Go on,' Ursula said.

Arm looked from woman to woman, their faces identically resolute, deadpan. Just like that, they had allied against him.

'Looks like my mind is made up for me,' he muttered and got up over the gate.

Rebecca laughed and tugged the rein, bringing the horse around.

'Okay, now, get on up on the side here . . . One foot in then throw yourself over. Don't be afraid to take hold of the mane.'

'She won't mind?' Arm asked.

'You can tug the shit out of it, it's fine,' Rebecca said. She had a calming hand on the horse's long jaw as Arm futzed to get on.

He toed his left foot into the stirrup on his side and stepped down until the strap went taut. He clutched a hank of horse hair and drew himself up towards the saddle, paddling air with his right leg until he'd groped it down the far side of the horse's flank. Then Arm was solidly astraddle, and gripping the pommel he pushed himself upright in the hard leather of the seat. In the transition from ground to back the horse seemed to have grown to twice its original size.

'Alright. I'm going to take you round, at walking pace first,' Rebecca said. 'I'll guide her with the reins, you just hold steady and relax. And don't fall off.'

'Look, look at your daft daddy,' Arm heard Ursula say.

Jack had his teeth sunk in the wooden fence. His eyes flicked dispassionately across the half-horse-half-daddy creature steadying itself in front of him.

Rebecca led Arm and the horse into the patchy turf of the open field. Arm was sent rocking, side to side, on the barrel of knit muscle beneath him. Then the horse began to move faster.

'Okay we're speeding up a bit now!' Rebecca shouted.

Arm watched her bouncing head of curls, saw the crooked white line bisecting her crown where the part in her hair naturally opened. Then the rein was not in her hand anymore. The horse's shoulder shot passed her. Its stride opened out. Arm bounced and bounced, skewing from side to side in the saddle. He tried to get his head up. Rebecca was gone, somewhere behind him. The reins were a loop of flimsy leather flickering along the side of the horse's straining head. Nephin Mountain hiccupped violently up and down in the air in front of him.

Arm pressed his face into the long swinging neck. He could smell the velvet mustiness of the creature's hide, the sweetness of the pulverised grass and black earth as it cut up under the thrumming hooves. 'Stop,' Arm was moaning, 'stop, stop, stop.'

He thought of Fannigan, pale as any apparition, a body riding the current to sea.

They were heading towards the fence on the far side, and it was only at the last moment that the horse banked and swung around in an arc, shooting back the way it had come. Rebecca was standing in the middle of the field, arms up and out, furiously flagging them down. The horse beelined for her and decelerated to a choppy trot.

Rebecca snatched the dangling reins and pulled the horse's head down. This had an effect as instantaneous as putting a car into neutral. Now the animal ambled at a desultory clip, and after the burst of speed it felt to Arm as if he were floating. He was loose-boned, adrenalised and softly tittering at a high, wretched pitch that sounded like it was coming from somewhere else. The bolt into the wind had driven tears from his eyes.

'What was that move? You shot off there like the Lone Ranger!' Ursula exclaimed, her hand on the back of Jack's neck. He still had his jaws locked into the fence.

'Fuck, sorry man,' Rebecca said. 'She just spooked.'

'I didn't do anything,' Arm exclaimed, to both women.

'You didn't mean to,' Rebecca corrected him, 'I shouldn't have had you up there. Normally it's only me or the kids on her. You smell and weigh like a different species. Sorry, Douglas. Get on down.'

'It's alright,' Arm said, 'I'm fine.'

And dignified as he could, he poured the shook jelly of himself off the beast.

'You could've broken your neck,' Ursula mused brightly.

Arm winced at her, then rested his elbows on the fence and tipped his forehead onto his crossed wrists. In the little hollow comprised of his arms and head and chest he listened for his racing heart to come back down to an even keel. Arm knew if he raised either hand out flat in the air it would be shaking. A tear loosed itself from a lash and hit his cheek, running down his skin in a hot stripe.

Rebecca was somewhere behind him, near. Arm could feel her looking at him.

'You ever get knocked out in the ring?' she said, as if she was following exactly his thoughts and wanted to change tack.

Arm shook his head where it lay.

'I didn't think so,' she said.

'Lots of hits,' Arm said, swabbing his eyes. 'But I was never truly put out.'

'I'll get him home, if you want,' Arm said to Ursula. 'I'll take him up to Supermacs for a Coke and burger first.'

'Shouldn't be encouraging him to eat that shite,' Ursula said.

'Well. He's a little boy. They like rubbish.'

Rebecca was patting the horse's grey face. 'I got to get this brat fed and watered,' she announced. 'We have a convoy coming in from the retirement home just after lunch.'

'Good luck with that,' Arm said. 'Hope that fecker doesn't throw you.'

'She won't,' Rebecca said, 'I'll see you next week, Jack.'

Jack pulled his mouth away from the fence. There was a blotch of saliva, a bracelet of bite marks worried into the wood.

Arm shepherded Jack up the main street. Jack knew where they were going and was getting excited, yipping and wanting to scramble ahead. Arm kept a finger snagged in the collar of his jacket.

'Walk,' he urged, 'Walk.'

Dympna rang.

'How's the head, soldier?'

'Not bad,' Arm said. 'Just out with the boyeen.'

'I've a soft skin on me today, myself. Jesus Christ, we were milling through that whiskey like it was water,' Dympna chuckled. He sounded supine and pleasantly shattered. Dympna enjoyed stewing in his hangovers, and often passed entire afternoons in a recuperative fog on the living-room sofa, duvet crimped around his neck like a barber's bib, downing two-litre bottles of Fanta and watching box set after box set of DVDs.

'Out with Jackie boy, is it?'

'Correct,' Arm said.

'When's that done up?'

'Shortly.'

'Cool, cool, sure I can drop down and grab you.'

'It's okay.'

'I know its okay, it's no bother,' he said. 'We'd best get out there, get things squared up.'

When Arm did not respond Dympna said, 'Sorry, fuck. Look. Take your time with Jackie.'

'I didn't say anything,' Arm said.

'You have grades of brooding silence, Arm,' Dympna said, 'I can tell I pissed you off, or else you already were. Either way I'm not adding to it. We both have enough shite on our plates.'

'And sometimes you have to eat it up,' Arm said.

'Exactly,' Dympna said. 'And speaking of which. Fannigan. Don't sweat on that.'

'I wasn't,' Arm said.

'The uncles we can bring round. We can get them to see what's best in the long run.'

'You didn't think so last night.'

'Ah, I was drunk. Letting fretfulness get the better of me,' Dympna said, like it was all nothing. 'So. Will swing down your way for four, will we say? Give you plenty a time with the lad.'

'Okay.'

'I know,' Dympna sighed, 'it just goes on and on, doesn't it?'

'It does.'

Arm still had his finger hooked in Jack's coat collar. They were at the zebra crossing. A modest stream of traffic was emptying down the main street. Cloudbanks blotted the sun above the post office and the air was laced with a salt foretaste of rain.

Jack lurched forward, impatient to cross. He could not see or register or interpret the flashing bodies of the passing vehicles, they were not even ghosts to him.

'Nyyhhh,' Jack was moaning. 'Nyyhhh, NYYHHH.'

He was building up a head of steam, and slapped himself, openhanded, on the side of his head.

'Stop,' Arm said, and put his hand over that part of Jack's head. Jack slapped again, hit the buffer of Arm's hand, then dug his nails into Arm's skin. After five seconds whatever possessed him subsided, he pulled his nails free, and within ten he was burbling happily again.

In Supermacs Arm and Jack took the booth nearest the entrance, the booth they always took. It was Saturday but the place was swarming with convent girls—they were in doing weekend study, Arm guessed, and had descended here on their lunch break, and now they milled and ate and chatted in a chaos of perfume and high voices, a chorus of mobiles chirping and bleeping around them. Jack ate his chips one by one, as he always did, before attending to his burger. Six girls were squished into the adjacent booth, practically spilling into each other's laps. A couple of them were shyly watching Jack. He took the top bun from the burger, held the inside up to his face and, moving it circumferentially in front of his gob, licked every last particle of ketchup and grease from it, then replaced the bun back on the untouched patty. And that was that, that was Jack's version of eating a burger. Arm heard the girls laugh then stop themselves, and without eyeing the culprits he managed a smile. Arm wanted them to know it was okay; they had permission to find Jack funny. Because he was, he was a funny fucker.

*   *   *

Arm told Ursula he would take Jack to the horses next time, to watch the boy ride firsthand. They were in the kitchen, Ursula smashing eggs against the porcelain lip of a mixing bowl, seesawing the yolk back and forth between each shell-half until the clear glop had run off.

'I bet you will,' she said.

'Did I or did I not get up on that beast? I want to see Jack do it.'

'Uh-huh,' she said. 'Standing there silent, with the legs out,' she braced her hips and mimicked Arm's stance. 'You think you're a solid block of charm, huh?'

Their exchange was accompanied by a succession of muffled bangs going off around their heads. Jack had shed his trousers, scaled the washing machine and was now taking a tour of the countertop that ran along two walls of the kitchen, skipping adroitly over the cutting board and microwave and toaster, attempting to pry open the safety-locked door of every wall-mounted cupboard and press.

'Got to head,' Arm said, 'bye, Jack.'

Bang on four Arm was at the usual pickup spot, the pebble-dashed wall of the petrol station at the foot of his estate. He rested his tailbone against the wall, plugged in his headphones, and watched the road for the shit-box. After a while it appeared, the inimitable lump of Dympna's silhouetted head rocking to and fro in the windshield. Dympna pulled up, popped the passenger door and sunk back into the driver seat. He was wrecked, scalp shining, cheeks mottled with lividity. A half-empty bottle of Fanta was wedged at an angle between the front seats, behind the hand brake. Dympna lifted it, took a guzzle, violently massaged his eyes and brow.

'Sorry I'm late,' Dympna lamented, 'a drained head on me and then them women start up. Them women. Don't even ask me to get into it. There's always something.'

'No worries,' Arm said.

'I'm in no humour for this,' Dympna said. 'But then I guess no humour at all is the best humour to be in to deal with these fucking Indians.'

They were clear of the town within minutes. They sped past the red-roofed, white-walled barns and holds of the farms just beyond the town limits, past lopsided fields where sheep drifted like flocks of grounded, flea-bitten clouds.

'Maybe,' Arm said. 'Will Hector be back?'

'From throwing the monthly length into the woman? Doubt that now.'

'So it'll just be the other fella.'

'That's what the maths'd tell us,' Dympna said, letting rip a bassy, gaseous belch. He drove in the typical town-boy manner, seatbeltless and slouched back in his seat, the heel of a palm propped against the wheel while with his other hand he alternated between palming open his mobile to check for texts and taking regular hits off the Fanta.

'They're gearing up for another bout of being difficult,' he said. 'Like fucking teenagers. Volatile.'

'You might be right.'

'That's what the Fannigan business is about. Like they give a shit about Charlie or any of us. It's an excuse to start up on me, on us. With that in mind, you might come in.'

'Into the house?'

'Yeah, sit down there with me and Paudi. Give him what you call a show a solidarity.'

'You scared?' Arm said.

'Scared? Of a couple of auld lads?' Dympna laughed. 'Arm, you are the scariest man I know, considered coldly. You could put me in a coma, bare-handed, in two minutes flat, and most everyone else around. But I'm not scared of you, how could I be?'

Dympna glugged his Fanta.

They were beyond the farmsteads now, into reefs of bogland infested with gorse bushes. Bony, hard-thorned and truculently thriving, the gorse bushes' yellow blossoms were vivid against the grained black sheen of the sump waters, the seamed bog fields. The sky was clearing itself of clouds. The day was on its afternoon wane, already.

'It's getting on,' Arm said.

'Just sit there and say nothing,' Dympna said. 'Just sit there and be, y'know, intimidating.'

'I can manage that.'

The road into the farm was a narrow length of rutted dirt sunk low between haggard ditches. They had to crawl over the track, the shitbox pitching up and down as they went. The farm itself backed out onto a hill thick with heather. The house was a T-shaped unpainted wooden bungalow with a sagging front porch. A wrought-iron gate, hingeless, was tethered by an inordinate quantity of blue rope to the porch's frame, though the gate still hung at a limp angle.

They parked in the clearing out front.

Paudi came round the side of the house. He had a baseball cap scrunched down over his head and his beard was as lush as ever, a streaked dark thicket that devoured his neck and three quarters of his face. He was standing in rakey profile, watching the car and cleaning his hands with the end of his T-shirt.

Dympna slapped the roof of the shitbox as he got out.

'Well, Unk,' he said, 'fine cunt of a day and no mistake.'

'Come see this,' Paudi said, turning and disappearing back behind the house. Arm looked at Dympna, shrugged his shoulders. Dympna popped the shitbox's boot, slung the satchel containing the uncles' cut over his shoulder.

Behind the house a courtyard of cracked concrete led to the cattle shed. The shed was decently cavernous, a three-sided, aluminium-walled structure with a gated front and a corrugated roof. It was no longer used to house livestock, but was now a repository for an accumulation of all manner of weathered and defective shite—a capsized washing machine, two fat-backed cathode TVs with their screens smashed out, yards of dismembered PVC and metal piping, tyres of varying circumferences and vehicle type, cardboard trays containing broken, esoterically shaped glassware and fertiliser bags full of a mixture of wood shavings and small brown pellets of what might have been animal feed but could've been anything. To the rear of the shed was the cellar door that led down, Arm knew, to the nursery, and beside that door was the pair of wire cages in which were kept the Alsatians. One sprung to its feet and pressed its shining muzzle against the mesh, beads of slaver dropping from its teeth onto the mesh's squares. The other creature remained curled into itself in the corner of its cage.

'Look at this poor bastard,' Paudi said.

The dog's snout was buried under its front paws, its breath coming in rapid, shallow rasps. It was lying on a bath mat, the mat's ends filigreed with chew-marks.

'What's up with it?' Dympna said.

'He ate a wasp. It's a habit they've had since they were pups. Wasps do nest up in the eaves of the porch every summer, and after me or the other fella get round to killing them these boys love to snuffle round the deck and eat up the bodies. Think he ate one he thought was dead wasn't dead. Stung him, it did, inside in his throat or deeper down. His tongue is all fucked up and he's been wheezing and stuck lying there since yesterday. Can dogs be allergic?'

'You have me there,' Dympna said. 'This happened yesterday?'

'Correct. Did Hector not tell you?' Paudi took ahold of one of the longer curls depending from the end of his beard and rolled it between his thumb and forefinger.

'No,' Dympna said.

'Well fuck that goon,' Paudi said, starting back around for the front of the house.

Paudi led them into the front room.

'You put in a word to the vet yet?' Dympna asked.

'We'll see,' Paudi said. 'Sit down.'

The front room was tiny. There was a fireplace in the wall, a copper bucket brimming with ashes by the hearth, a metal shovel sunk free-standing in the ash, so thick was the deposit of it. The flock wallpaper had warped and bubbled in the corners, like the room had been parboiled. Paudi's chair had a layer of old newspapers tucked around the lining of the seat; the papers served as a kind of supplementary padding and crackled as he settled himself.

Dympna scooted onto the leather fainting couch, leaving Arm to a puny, three-legged wooden stool. Arm turned and descended upon it. Achieving a tremulous emplacement, he found he had nowhere to put his arms but heaped atop his thighs.

Paudi looked at him, snickered.

'Sometimes a big man can't do nothing but sit there and be fucking big, hah?'

The table was a small, fold-down plastic number. A shopping bag containing the latest consignment of weed sat on it. Dympna placed the satchel on the table, next to the shopping bag. Paudi did not unzip or otherwise inspect the satchel beyond giving the leather a gentle squeeze. He looked at Arm.

'Is your boy better?' he said.

Dympna raised his hand but said nothing. His eyes darted from Arm to Paudi, then back to Arm.

'My boy?'

'The little lad. Your little fella. The one can't talk.'

'It's not a case of him getting better.'

Paudi considered this.

'But he's trainable, yes? If that's the word.'

134

'He is, I suppose.'

'He's a great lad,' Dympna said blandly.

'You never brought young Armstrong in before,' Paudi said, addressing Dympna, 'that's a new thing.'

'And what's it matter?' Dympna said.

'It's an observation,' Paudi said. 'Yes sir.'

Then he said, 'I cannot believe Hector did not tell you about the dog. All that man cares about is his little bit snuck away in Ballintober.'

'Women,' Dympna muttered.

'She has him under her spell,' Paudi said. 'He thinks he has her under his. But it's the other way round. His brain is turning to mush, you know. The man has an unconscionable stack of sprays and perfumes sat in there by the bed.' A horizontal crease spread in the middle of his beard. Paudi was smiling. 'He baths himself every second day. He has these little nail clippers. He wants nothing to do with the silage. He forgets to feed the fucking dogs,' he concluded coldly.

'But sure the one out there will be fine anyway,' Dympna said. 'They eat anything, they have constitutions of iron.'

'I will have to take it for a walk up the heather it if does not look like she's improving,' Paudi said. 'It's a pity. But that's fucking that.'

'That'll be too bad,' Dympna said.

'But what's this development about though?' Paudi said. His hand returned to the satchel. He pinched a fold of the thin imitative leather between his yellow fingers. 'You know I'm up here on my own. And in you bring the Arm.'

'He's just my lad,' Dympna said. 'A loyal skin.'

'Loyal skin,' Paudi repeated. 'Loyalty among thieves, isn't that the saying?'

'Is it?' Dympna said. 'Well, say whatever you like, Paudi, consider me him and him me when it comes to our business.'

'Speaking of projects, Valentino was on to you yesterday, yes?' Paudi shifted his weight in his chair, the papers crackling around his thighs. 'What's the story with the molester?'

'You mean Fannigan?' Dympna said.

'Another loyal skin, no doubt,' Paudi smiled again. 'You're drowning in loyal skins, nephew.'

'Fannigan is dead,' Arm said.

Dympna laughed, a single dry bark.

'Just so you know,' Arm said.

Paudi tweaked the curl in his beard.

'Really?' Paudi said.

Arm stood up. He put his hand in his pocket and threw the blood-flecked stone out onto the table. It skittered to a stop against the satchel.

'There you go. There's a biteen of his fucking brains still stuck to that.'

Paudi picked up the stone. He turned it over in his hand.

Dympna forced out another laugh, this one huskier, faker. 'He's messing with you,' he said, his voice on the verge of cracking.

'Messing,' Paudi said.

'I'm not,' Arm said.

Paudi looked up at Arm. 'He's not, either.'

Paudi oriented the stone until he had it set into the concave space between his thumb and forefinger. He held it like he was going to throw it, forefinger doubled tight against the stone's curve, to maximise torque and spin. Then he threw it square between Arm's eyes.

Dympna let out a yell. Arm snapped his head back and put his hand to the bridge of his nose. Dympna and Paudi stood up simultaneously and then all three men made their moves. Half-blind, Arm reached out and took a grip of someone's shoulder. The shoulder recoiled from him and Dympna went facedown over the table. The table collapsed and his whirling foot snagged the handle of the bucket by the fireplace, launching it into the air. It crashed to the earth in a plume of flurrying brown ash. Arm stepped sideways, barked a shin against the table's edge. He was coughing; Dympna was coughing. Arm was trying to get himself facing where he thought Paudi was when Paudi spoke, his breath against Arm's ear.

'Stop now.'

Dympna righted himself and got to his feet. Waving his hands, he attempted to bat clear the pall of flitting, granular ash. He squinted through the pall at his uncle.

'Is that a fucking gun?' he said.

'It is,' Paudi said. Paudi had his back against the wall, the muzzle of a double-barrelled rifle pointing towards Arm and Dympna, its wooden butt tight against his hip-bone. Arm looked at Dympna and tried to gauge from his expression how serious he should take the gun. Dympna was wearing a wan smile, as was Paudi, and for a moment it seemed as if the entire situation was no more than a momentary domestic awkwardness uncle and nephew were conspiring to prolong out of some pique of mutual amusement.

But Paudi kept the rifle levelled at them.

'Easy, horse,' Paudi said to Arm. Arm was rubbing his nose, blood coming from the bridge where the stone had hit.

'Paudi. Come on. What the fuck?' Dympna said, tight-jawed.

'I know what this is,' Paudi said.

Paudi's black eyes were shiny, charged, grimly tabulating.

'The Arm. The quiet man,' Paudi spat. Whenever the muzzle passed Arm's gut he felt everything inside him turn to air. 'Ready to pounce at the drop of a hat.'

'Ah now, what? What the fuck are you saying?' Dympna said.

'Step out, both of you,' Paudi said.

They moved carefully backwards out onto the porch and onto the unevenly grassed earth. It was still warm and bright outside.

'Hands up,' Paudi said.

Dympna and Arm complied.

'This is a mix up, Paudi,' Dympna insisted, but there was no conviction in his voice. Arm knew that Paudi would not listen, or would listen, but not back down.

'You're out of your fucking mind,' Arm threw in, anyway.

'Nah,' Paudi said mildly. He went quiet for a moment, then, addressing Arm: 'You killed that Fannigan fella, just like that, hah? What do you think you are?'

'I'm not anything,' Arm assured him.

'Yeah, yeah, yeah. You've shown your hand,' Paudi said.

'It was you boys wanted Fannigan dealt with. It was the other fat cunt showed up yesterday saying how Dympna's old man wouldn't want to let this lie,' Arm said.

'Invoking the dead,' Paudi tittered. 'That'd be Heck alright.'

'Fuck all that!' Dympna shouted, 'What about this? You thought, what? We came here to do you over and fucking what? Rob you?'

Paudi did not respond.

Arm was standing with his hands up and out either side of his head. Dympna had his fingers interlinked, palms on his crown, rocking his elbows demonstrably in the air as he spoke.

'So what's going to happen, Unk?' Dympna said.

Paudi spat.

Arm looked above the porch, past the roof. Back of them, he estimated, there were thirty or more feet of open ground to cover to get to the shitbox. Arm could smell the heather and could see, beyond the house, the upper part of the hill, the graded billows of green and brown and purple fronds turning languidly in the wind, then turning back again. Beyond the hill's crest a tiny plane slipped frictionlessly across the sky, shedding a wake of thin white exhaust that feathered apart as it hung there, in the grey.

Thirty feet. Give or take. It was too far, Arm knew. If this man was actually going to use the gun he'd get every chance no matter how lightning they ran.

And so the three stayed put, just silent and waiting. The uncle regarded the two. Arm heard Dympna let out a deep breath.

'Ah now, Unk,' Dympna said, 'fuck all this for a game of soldiers.'

Dympna dropped his arms and started forwards, stepping right up to Paudi and closing the substantial meat of his palm over the barrel, nudging the muzzle downwards.

The noise was there and gone, a slap to the air that left it hot and thrumming. Arm was jarred, punch-drunk, blood droning thickly in his ears. The Alsatians were off, barking dementedly out back, one or both, maybe. The bridge of Arm's nose throbbed. He blinked to water away the sudden flecks of grit inundating his eyes. His face was very hot. There was a smell. Dympna was genuflecting on one knee in the grass. His sleeve was mostly gone and a gouge of black and red smoked along the underside of his arm, wrist to elbow. Dympna's sleeve was in tatters. He was still holding the double barrel. The smell was the smell of combusted flesh. Dympna's arm was bad but there was also his leg. Paudi stepped back and the gun barrel slid from Dympna's grip. Dympna made a fist with his other hand, his left, and bowled a hopeless swing in the direction of his uncle. The momentum brought Dympna keeling forward. The shot leg seemed to stay upright a moment longer, then it too capsized, dragged by the portion of it that was still connected to Dympna's thigh.

Arm turned and ran, lunging so quickly from a standing position he felt his right hamstring tear within a

couple of strides, but he kept going. He fell against the
driver door. The keys were in the ignition. The engine
whinnied like a piteous bitch. Arm was stepping on the
clutch like it was Paudi's windpipe. He put the shitbox
in gear and commenced turning. Dympna was down so
low on the ground Arm could not see him over the bonnet. But Paudi was moving, circling in behind the shitbox
as Arm trundled for the gap to the track out of there.
Paudi loped, the rakey fucker, right into Arm's blind spot.
The door window on Arm's side caved in. Arm punched
the shitbox through the gap and hit the lane. The ruts
attacked the suspension with such violence his jaw
slammed shut on his tongue. Brambles from the ditch
threshed in through the window. Shards of glass bounced
like loose change all over his legs.

Arm careened out onto the road, slew a vicious right
angle towards town and ground into third. Away, away,
he was away. Arm could not tell if he was going fast or
slow.

He thought: *Dympna.*

He thought: *I have got away.*

He thought: *Bullshit.*

Keeping the lurching, shifting shitbox on the road was
his immediate concern. The wind whistled in through
the shattered window. He moved his right arm and a
scalding pain lanced up through his torso. The pain stuck.
Arm felt impaled, run through.

This was a thing to worry about. But not yet.

He drove, trying to keep his right side still. His hamstring burned. Arm had to take periodic gulps of the
blood leaking from his tongue. The gorse bushes in the

bog fields juddered in the wind. Arm joggled switches until the headlights snapped bright, and kept his eyes locked on the immediate section of macadam refreshing itself in the windshield.

No other cars appeared. Arm assured himself that Paudi was not in pursuit. How could he be? The uncles had only the one road vehicle, a Hiace van, and it was in Ballintober where Hector was dallying with his widow.

Arm tried to assess the situation, but what was there to assess? Things had got fucked, precipitously and in multiple ways, and for little reason. Arm had come to this place with Dympna. Arm and Dympna had entered Paudi's house. Arm had informed Paudi he had done away with someone Paudi and his brother had asserted they wanted done away with, and Paudi had interpreted this as what? A dry-run for what he thought Arm and Dympna were about to do to him? The paranoid fucks. It was always going to come asunder like this.

The homely glimmer of the town lights appeared ahead. Arm eased in along the main road. Coming up ahead was the turnoff for the town farm. Arm could not risk driving the beat-up shitbox through Main Street. He figured the farm would serve as well as anyplace to stow the shitbox and consider his damage. The rider, Rebecca, would surely be gone by now, along with whatever other staff there was.

Arm swung up the lane into the farm parking lot. He parked in a corner, far as he could from any streetlights. He cut the engine, rested his forehead against the wheel, careful not to set off the horn. Midges moved in through the window and strafed his scalp. It was getting cooler. When Arm lifted his head the evening seemed darker again. He experimentally tried his right arm. Bringing his elbow to the level of his collarbone made the pain squeeze Arm's chest so hard he had to catch his breath. The seat was wet, and squelched as Arm peeled himself from it.

He hobbled across the lot, a hunchbacked crook to his gait that sufficed to dampen, just a little, the pains in his torso and leg. The moon was out, a little early, it seemed to Arm. At the cottage door a sensor light ticked on. He knocked the pansies from the sill as he squinnied through the window. Empty.

Arm shouldered the door until it gave, and stepped into the tiny office. There was a foldout chair behind a plywood desk only a little bigger than a bedside locker, a kitchenette in the corner. There was a microwave on the counter, a waxy braid of noodles slopped in a plastic beaker. On the desk was a ring-bound ledger, a row of identical ledgers lined a shelf behind the desk, and a fashion magazine with a cigarette dook scorched through a model's face. Arm sat. He pulled off his shirt and inspected the back. It was drenched in a swathe of syrupy, sticky stuff turned dark plum against the denim, and perforated by a scatter of grim little holes. He climbed arm by arm back into the shirt and sat back down into the chair. He closed his eyes and waited to see if he would die or at least pass out. Five minutes later and nothing had happened. In fact Arm was feeling only hungry, ravenous. He nuked the stale noodles for twenty seconds in the

microwave and ate them with his bare hands, fingerpaint-
ing the polystyrene container with his blood.

There was a locked drawer attached to the desk. Arm
held the table to keep it steady and pulled the drawer
right out of its fixture. Inside was a quantity of the rider's
effects. Her full name, Rebecca Mileacre, appeared over
and over on a folded stack of crumpled wage slips, along
with the pittance they were paying her.

'Mileacre,' Arm said.

There was a small red tin box. Arm split it open against
the table. It contained a pile of coppers and one hundred
and seventy-five quid in loose notes. Petty cash. On a
hook behind the door was an army surplus coat. It smelled
of hay, dung, horsehide, the rider.

Arm stepped out into the air. He thought about the
first time he came here and why, and felt a pang of remorse
that he had never seen Jack on horseback as he'd originally intended.

In an open-topped sty a dozen pigs were crammed
contentedly together, slumbering. Their plump pale bodies shuddered as snores ripped ebulliently from their
blunt, electrical-socket-shaped snouts. There was a
chicken coop with a mesh perimeter, the coop completely
silent by contrast, and beyond that the barn the horse was
kept in. Arm unlatched the gate and retreated a respectful
distance. The barn was a cubular blot of darkness, of
uncertain depth and reeking of oats and horseshit. After
a moment, the horse itself clackingly emerged from its
nest of shadows.

'Not so spooked now?' Arm said.

He proffered a hand, held it neutrally in the air. The beast twitched its head then went still. Its stillness was its consent. Arm brushed his palm against the grain of its snout, felt the heat fluming from the vents of its nostrils. A vein thick as a garden hose pulsed among the muscles of its white neck.

'You know me, now,' Arm said.

He opened the gate and the animal drifted out into the middle of the field. Arm followed at a respectful distance. It hurt to breathe and it hurt not to breathe, and it was getting harder to register the distinction. The horse snuffled, swished its tail and pricked its ears, sifting the air for emanations beyond Arm's ken. Eventually he cottoned that it was looking right at Nephin Mountain.

Arm thought of Dympna genuflecting, the sudden teetering ruin of his body. He thought of Dympna sliding into the grass. Arm could not imagine the moment beyond that moment; because there was none, none he could stand.

It seemed years ago that the sun was in the sky and he and Dympna had tooled out to the uncles in the faithful shitbox of the Corolla, cool and contained and helplessly complacent in their schemes. Thinking all along they had sufficient quantities of neck, gall and brains to treat with those odd birds, to bend the uncles to the inclination of their wills.

Dympna in the grass. Arm thought of the seven sisters, the mother June, formidable as a mountain range, watching their men go away. Arm wanted to tell them all sorry, and saw himself standing in their front room, empty-handed and dripping blood into the carpet; trying to get the words out, each utterance dropping from his mouth like a dead black wasp.

The horse trotted off and came back. Arm put out his hand. The horse's snout skimmed in along the flat of his palm, muzzle steaming. Bands of moon sheen slid across its hide.

'Come on,' Arm said, and led the creature back to its stable. He returned to the cottage and took the rider's surplus jacket from the door. It just about fit. Arm buttoned it up, took the petty cash and went out to the shitbox.

It was a half-hour drive to Ballintober along a see-sawing, pothole-pocked road. Rows of reflective white stakes flanked the tight verge. The shitbox held up, and Arm came to feel as a reprieve the night blasting in through the shattered window. He did not know where the widow lived, knew only the family name, Mirkin, but figured he would not have to turn up too many stones before he happened upon her and Hector. Ballintober was a junction, a football pitch, a petrol station, post office and butchers, eight pubs, and a brushed aluminium road sign arrowed at the Dublin road. Arm selected the shabbiest looking pub, lurched inside, and the very first fellow he talked to was only too happy to supply directions. The rider's petty cash, which Arm thought he might require for a conversational sweetener, never left his pocket. The fellow was a pensioner in crusted wellies and an angling jacket, bright feathered fishhooks lining his breast pocket like army medals. He even offered to sketch out a map as the barman, an overweight bald lad in black, observed silently. Arm thanked the fellow and offered to buy him a pint, but the old sot demurred.

'Calling at this hour, you can only be up to no good,' he said. 'Good luck!'

The house was set in off the road, a hundred-yard drive leading into it. Tall trees lined the front and sides of the property like battlements. Arm motored slowly by, caught sight of a large, two-storied building. Ramshackle, spare, but with a ghostly stateliness in its bones. Down along the road Arm pulled into a boreen. His back had settled into a dull throb. It was still difficult to breathe, there was a nagging sensation of being continuously winded, but Arm wondered if he wasn't over the worst of it; that he had bled out all the blood he was going to.

He got out of the shitbox, left the dashlight on. He took a few steps down the boreen, tenderly squeezing his rent hamstring. The ache there was tolerable, though a sprint of any sort was out of the question.

On the other side of the ditch Arm could hear the big-bodied padding of cows, moving like barges through the long grass. Arm took out his mobile. The screen lit up, one bar of battery left. He thumbed through his contact list. He selected Dympna and pressed call. Arm could feel his heart as the line rang and rang out. Dympna's voicemail. *Spake and leave a message whoever you are, sham,* went his recorded voice, bored and dismissive sounding. There was a beep and then the thirty-second void into which Arm could have spoke.

The boreen was divided from the field by a ditch, but where the ditch's growth was not so hectic Arm could discern a wall beneath. The wall was comprised of interlocking lumps of stone, all buttressed, layered and balanced carefully against one another, unmortared, held in place purely by the tension of their placement, though some of the topmost rocks had fallen away. At a thin point in the ditch Arm scrabbled up the wall, found his footing at the apex and, from this point of elevation, considered the lay of the surround. The Mirkin house was three fields over, discernible only by patches of moon-bright whitewash through the perimeter of trees.

Two cows turned and shuffled towards him.

Arm looked to his phone again.

He scrolled down to URSULA D, last in the list as ever. Arm stared blackly at the lit screen and ground his teeth against the urge to call. Then he rang and Ursula, too, rang out. Arm cut off the voice mail and dialled again. On the second ring the connection clicked.

'Hello,' Ursula said.

'It's me.'

'Yes?' she said.

'I was just ringing to see how Jack was.'

A pause.

'He's fine,' she said with soft dubiety, as if she didn't quite recognise Arm's voice.

'Is he settled down for the night or still up?'

Another pause. This was not a usual thing, this call and questions.

'Douglas,' she said.

'Yeah.'

'He's up.' The way she said it, Arm knew the boy was within eyeshot, and perhaps Jack was looking at her as she spoke to Arm. Jack knew, most of the time, when he was being talked about, could pick out the taut monosyllable of his name in the otherwise mashed white noise of human conversation.

'It's getting on for him to be up,' Arm said.

'It's not that late,' Ursula said, elaborating guardedly, like their talk was a code. 'It'll be bath time any minute now.'

'And then bed,' Arm said.

'Then bed.'

'Good,' Arm said, relieved. 'What are you at now?'

'Me?'

'Yeah.'

Another hesitancy. Beneath the electronic burr of the connection there came faint background ructions. Arm pictured Jack monkeying bare-legged from nook to nook, hunting for scraps of bread.

'Nothing. A bit of washing,' she said. 'There's the usual fucking mountain to get through.'

'Sorry. Sorry for interrupting, like.'

'That's okay,' she said.

'Going to get a bit of study in tonight?' Arm said.

She cleared her throat. 'Might snatch a half hour alright, if I can be bothered.'

'You will. You should,' Arm said, as evenly and sincerely as he could. 'You'll get there in the end, you know.'

'I intend to,' she said, and then, 'Douglas, are you alright?'

Arm could hear the edge of a smile in her question. The call had blindsided her, put her on the defensive, but now, Arm supposed, she had decided that he was being merely harmlessly strange, and it bemused her.

'Yeah, no, I'm fine. I was just thinking. About nearly being killed on that fucking horse today.'

'Oh,' she said, and sniffed. 'Yeah. That was great.'

'It took some fucking turn against me.'

'Must be a good judge.'

'Leave off. You wouldn't have really wanted me to break my neck,' Arm said.

Ursula made a doubtful mmmm sound.

'Didn't think so,' Arm said, 'are you warming up to me again, girl?'

She tutted in mock disgust at the suggestion.

'You cut, Arm, is that it?'

'Look,' Arm said, 'I'm sorry I haven't been around.'

'You're never out of my hair,' Ursula singsonged.

'In a useful way,' Arm said. 'You deserve better.'

'Everyone deserves better, Douglas,' Ursula snapped, her voice tuned to a clear low. Her attention had flowed elsewhere again; Arm could tell her eyes were back on Jack.

'Maybe it'd be better the other way altogether, so.'

Arm heard her sigh. 'What's that mean?' she said.

'Nothing. Look. I'll leave you to it,' Arm said in a thick, drowned voice. He sounded faraway, even to himself.

'Okay, Douglas,' she said, and then, with a flicker of irritated puzzlement, 'Where are you, Arm? It's beyond quiet.'

'I'm outside. In a field. Watching cows watching me.'

'Right,' she said. 'Good luck with that.'

'Thanks.'

There was another silence. Then she said, 'Well, I'm best back to it here. Good night, so.'

'Bye,' Arm said as the line clicked off.

He went back to the shitbox. There was a toolbox in the boot, and in the toolbox a hammer. Arm clambered back up over the gap in the ditch and started across the fields.

Hector's Hiace was tucked round the side of the house, on Arm's side as he came up through the last field. Other than the stand of elms there was only a four-foot cement wall for a boundary, just about high enough to dismay a cow from trying to clotter over it. Arm limped quiet as he could through the yard. No dogs, thankfully. There was a light on in one of the downstairs rooms. The curtains were not pulled but there was a mesh drape. Arm went to the front door, knocked. There was no response for a time; he knocked again. Hector opened the door. He blinked and looked right at Arm.

'Your brother went fucking mad,' Arm said.

Hector went to close the door. Before he could Arm slugged him in the belly.

Hector bent, winded. Arm held the man's shoulder lest he fall over.

'Jaysus, Douglas,' Hector hissed, once he had regained his breath.

'You heard from him?' Arm said.

'Who?'

'Paudi,' Arm said, 'in the last whileen.'

'What? Paudi? No.'

151

'Who's there?' came a woman's voice from inside.

'I'm coming in,' Arm said. He had the hammer wedged down the back of his trousers. He pulled it out and pressed the prongs into Hector's cheek, then slipped it back down his arsecrack.

Hector winced, 'Douglas, whatever this is about we can talk again—'

'Give me a greeting,' Arm said, pushing Hector back and stepping inside the door. Up the hall drifted the pleasant smell of peatsmoke. The sitting room was in left, a set of stairs on the right. Hector, seeing he had no other option, recovered his composure and led Arm into the sitting room. Arm moved slowly to hide the hitch in his gait.

The widow Mirkin was standing at the fireplace, poker in hand, tending or affecting to tend to the big fire going in the hearth. Arranged upon her breast was a silver brooch with a greenish stone set in it. She was in a red and rust brown dress, one of those ones that showed nothing—the sleeves went down to the wrists, the blouse up to the neck, and the hemline descended comprehensively beyond the knees. Her hair was dark brown, raked back from her forehead and set in place with a simple, girlish band. She had no makeup on, a crow's-feet-riddled but decent face, Arm supposed, for an old dear. There was something faintly familiar about her, though beyond a certain age all old dears looked the same to Arm. The furniture, three chairs and a sofa, was festooned with corduroy cushions. The floor was carpeted, there was a crucifix on the wall, a framed portrait painting of a doe-eyed, winsome Christ. The fire spat and bubbled, the room was smotheringly warm.

'An acquaintance of yours, Hector?'

'By and by. He's a friend and associate of a young relative of mine, a nephew. Douglas, Maire. Maire, Douglas. He used to box for the county.'

The widow's eyes flicked over Arm, backed against the frame of the door.

'The carriage would suggest so, alright.'

'Did Hector not tell you I was coming over?' Arm said to her. 'He said it'd be okay.'

The widow looked inquiringly at her paramour. Hector was facing away from Arm, the bull neck above his collar empurpled and beaded with shine.

'Well, now, he did not.'

'My dear, I apologise for this,' Hector said.

She hooked the poker onto its stand by the hearth and stepped daintily into the middle of the room. She brought her hands together.

'Well you've intruded right into the middle of our nightcap, young man. I was just about to serve a toddy to Hector and myself. Can I fix you one? And sit down please, both of you.'

Hector turned to Arm and dropped into a chair. He gestured at the chair nearest Arm. Arm put himself in it, the rider's surplus jacket straining across his chest.

'Do,' Hector said to the widow, 'and cut us a few wodges of brack while you're at it, dear.'

The widow left for the kitchen.

Hector from his seat regarded Arm. He raised his hand to his mouth and nipped at a hangnail. 'Say what you have to,' he said in a mild voice, 'but say it low. She's to remain out of this.'

'Can't you send the biddy away?' Arm said.

Hector winced. 'It's her house, you fool.' He bared his teeth as if in pain and licked his lips. 'We could go, though, ladeen. We could go somewhere and sort this out.'

'Nah,' Arm said, sitting up. He could not get comfortable in the chair.

Hector's brow writhed in frustration. 'Please,' he said, 'let's not do this here.'

'She has money,' Arm said.

'What happened?'

'Today was delivery day. So we went out. As usual. But that brother of yours lost it, the mink. He whipped that rifle out at the drop of a hat. He brought a gun out on us, Heck.'

Hector's expression flickered through Arm, as if he was scrutinising something way off in the distance.

'Dympna,' Arm went on. 'He shot Dympna. He shot him. He, Shot, Him. Took a couple of potshots at me as I was getting out of dodge.'

'Where is Dympna now?' Hector said.

'He wasn't looking too healthy at all last I saw. Not at all last I saw. He took the brunt of that gun from less than a foot away.'

Hector swallowed a groan. He sat back and looked longingly at the fire blazing in the hearth, his wide face roseate.

'But this one has money, yeah?' Arm asked again.

Hector ran his hand down his leg and began absently rubbing the shin Arm had dinted.

'There's a nice lump blooming there already,' he said eventually. 'I need to talk to my fucking brother.'

'He's halfway to Timbuktu by now,' Arm said, 'or else he's fed himself a bullet. Either way he's leaving you up the Swanee.'

The widow returned, three steaming drinks on a silver tray and a couple of thick triangles of brack. She handed Arm a drink, a small plate, and placed a slice of the brack on the plate. Hector got the same treatment before she resumed her position, sentinel by the fireplace.

'Just the toddy for myself,' she announced.

'What's that smell?' Arm asked, holding the cup below his nose.

'Cloves,' she said. 'Have a taste.'

Arm nipped at it. 'Whiskey.'

'That's what a toddy is,' she said. 'Yours is not so strong as it only occurred to me in the kitchen that you must have driven across the county and will be soon enough driving back again, so I made it mild.'

She looked from Arm to Hector and smiled thinly.

'So this lad is not your relative? Maybe I'm biased but I think I see a bit of a resemblance.'

'No, no, my dear,' Hector said, summoning up a smile for his biddy. 'He merely works with my nephew. Our resemblances only extend as far as the fact we are both handsome men.'

'Well now, Hector, maybe that's it,' the widow Mirkin chortled, and Arm saw that she was in fact a little tipsy. She eyed Arm over her drink as she took a sup.

'Can I ask what the emergency was?'

Arm felt no particular urge to say anything. Hector looked at him and fumbled for words.

'There, well, it's only that it seems there may have been some kind of accident at the farm.'

'An accident?' the widow said gravely, her hand fluttering to her brooch. She looked from Hector to Arm.

'We may have to go, now, my dear,' Hector continued. 'Myself and Douglas, I mean. I don't want you concerned.'

'What on earth happened?' she asked.

'The nature of the incident is not, fully, ah, apparent yet,' Hector blustered, 'we're not sure how serious it is.' He balanced the plate of brack on his chair's armrest and stood up. Arm left down the victuals and shot to his feet too, a bolt of pain crackling through his middle.

'Hector, what is the matter?' the widow demanded. Hector girded himself and stepped forward. 'Let's just fucking go, Douglas,' he growled, bustling crabwise past Arm, chest out but a cringe distorting his face, like Arm might go for him. Hector stepped out into the frame of the door.

'Take another step yonder and I'll break both your fucking ankles, Heck,' Arm said.

Arm thought the widow might shriek or otherwise take fright at this articulation, but she was gazing in a spellbound way at the chair he had stepped out of. Her face was white, her expression shrunken.

'What has happened to you?' she said in a frail voice.

Arm looked back at the chair. A purplish stain had soaked down into the seat.

'Oh, God in heaven, you do not look well. You are not well,' the widow said.

'Maire Mirkin,' Arm said, 'I am sorry. I am on your premises under false pretences. But if I am, then so too is this sidling cunt in the jumper.' Out came the hammer and Arm pointed it towards Hector. Hector's face had gone tight, clotted.

'Hector,' the widow said.

'Maire Mirkin,' Arm continued, 'What does this fraud do? Show up with flowers, smile and charm. Throw a few quid your way to keep the house in trim, buy a nice thing or two in town. Well he has been playing you for a fool. His kind is poisonous. You've been letting a snake in through your door.'

The widow was staring at Hector, but she was listening to Arm.

'He wants your money,' Arm said.

'Money,' the widow said.

'Yes. The money. The money. Now go and get it,' Arm said.

'Money,' she said again.

'Yes. Money,' Arm said. 'Whatever's on the premises. In the attic, under the mattress, sewn into the bed linen, I couldn't give a fuck where it's hid, Maire, whether it's cash or coppers or gold or silver, but go and get it for me.'

Hector took a step towards Arm. 'You thick fucking daft cunt. You fucking loaf. Money! You think she has money!'

Arm dashed forward and grabbed Hector's arm, pulling downwards. Hector went unbalanced to his knees and Arm stepped around behind him. With a push he sent Hector sprawling chest forward onto the carpet and planted the knee of his good leg between Hector's shoulder blades, pinning him. Hector began shouting indecipherably into the carpet's thick weave. Arm grabbed a wrist, dragged Hector's arm clear of his body and brought the hammer whistling square down onto the back of his hand.

Hector screamed, a long guttural rent right into the carpet's fur. He thrashed about, but Arm kept his knee wedged steadily, even as the hamstring of his placed leg tautened and burned. Hector's convulsions jittered into sputtering stillness. He lifted his face up from the floor and twisted it sideways. His cheek was imprinted with pinpricks from the carpet fibres.

'Maire,' he sobbed.

Arm smacked him twice under the ear with the butt of the hammer's handle and pressed his elbow down onto Hector's neck. Arm still held Hector's hand. A purple squash-ball-sized bruise was bloating up off the skin with incredible rapidity and the rest of it was trembling limply, a misshapen nest of crazed nerves and pulverised bone.

'Now,' Arm said. There was a space between the end of the couch and the wall, and the widow had folded herself in there like a child playing hide and seek. She was looking at Arm.

'You want my money,' she said.

'That's all,' Arm said.

She unclasped the brooch on her dress and held it out to Arm.

'That's a start,' Arm said, and motioned for her to place it on the ground in front of her.

'The money,' she said. 'Mam only died a few weeks back. Mam was ill for a long time.'

'Maire,' Arm said. 'Maire. Are you listening? Things have gone bad here but we are going to make them right.'

She nodded dumbly, her eyes quaking. Hector was moaning softly, and had ceased struggling, immobilised but for the galvanic sputtering of his smashed hand. Arm dropped it loose and Hector sobbed again.

'Forget this fiend,' Arm said. And behind the fear Arm could see in the widow's eyes the beginning of an understanding. She knew Arm was not lying to her; the man on the floor had indeed brought him here.

'Get up,' Arm said. 'Get up, Miss Mirkin, and let's go get that money.'

'The money,' she giggled abruptly, scrambling to cover her mouth.

Arm disengaged his knee from Hector's elbow and got up. The widow gathered her skirt in and climbed to her feet. Arm stepped out of the way of the door to let her pass.

'No need for more commotion,' Arm said.

She stepped mindfully over Hector and into the hall. Arm followed.

'You cunts,' Hector slurred from the floor. The widow winced in distaste.

'Rest assured,' Arm told her, 'he brought this on himself.'

From the hall the widow regarded the sitting room, her expression moony, aqueous and fatigued. She

159

turned to Arm. Very gingerly she reached for his torso. Her touch was ice cold, for all the time she had spent by the fire.

'You're hurt,' she said, drawing back and displaying to Arm the tips of her blood-tipped fingers.

'I'm in fucking bits,' he admitted.

Now she looked towards the stairs, the steps ascending into the house's upper gloom.

'My mother passed up there,' she said. 'They let us take her home when she was close. Her room is still hers, all her things in it, exactly as it was.'

'Is that where it is?' Arm said. He had one eye on the stairs, one eye on the sitting room. Hector remained an inert heap on the floor.

The widow struggled to control her twitching lips. In a small voice she said, 'What if there is no money?'

'But there is,' Arm said, 'now take me up.'

'It's up there,' she said.

'Show me,' he said.

Her eyes welled. She issued a prim sniff of her nose. 'And this money,' she said. 'If I give it to you it will make something right? It will stop all this?'

Arm thought again of the moment to come, standing in the Devers's house, facing the scrutiny of June and Lisa and Charlie and the others, admitting to Dympna's fate and his abandonment of him. Something had to be done, one way or the other; something had to be done that Arm could stand to call reparation.

'It will help,' he said.

Hand on the banister, the widow took two uncertain steps up and turned back to him.

'This isn't you,' she said. 'It's a path you've ended up on, but it's not you.'

Arm sensed he had to be careful. The widow was brave enough to know she was imperilled and so was capable of audacity. He would have liked to believe her. Beyond the witchy severity, she had a kind face, and Arm realised who it was she reminded him of; the two women, the carers, fretting around trying to corral the kids the day he first went down to the town farm to see the horses. And that put Arm in mind of Jack. He thought of his son on the monkey bars, kissing the weathered painted metal and delightedly unleashing his eerie hoots and hollers, the ecstasy of the boy's utter seclusion.

The widow was leaning close. 'You are in bits,' she said, with tender insinuation. 'You need a minute. Lie down and take a minute, Douglas, you look like you are dying. Take a minute and think this through.'

'All I do is think,' Arm told her.

She seized his arm, 'You've done nothing yet.'

Arm took her wrist and twisted back. The widow gasped and stumbled backwards onto the steps. Holding her hand she looked with gaunt toylike impassivity up into Arm's face. He wanted to ask her what it was she saw there, but before he could she broke into a sob, and more sobs followed. She tried to choke them off but they prevailed in sputters, like raspy, tortured laughter. It is always an unseemly thing, Arm thought, to see someone you do not know break down crying.

'We're almost done.'

'You've done nothing,' she repeated, 'you've done nothing can't be turned back.'

Arm put out his hand, a politeness. He held it there and waited for her. What else could she do? The widow took it, and together they went up the stairs.

In the room the widow's hand trembled over the switch and turned on the light. There was a wide bed with a thick cover of patterned brocade, a metallic shimmer to the weave. Arm stood over it and looked down into the pattern, like looking into a body of water. Minute rucks littered the cover's surface.

'Sit down, sit down,' the widow's voice said.

Arm did. He let the hammer trail from his hand. The bedcover was cool, though sitting engendered another explosive jolt of pain through his sternum. Arm gritted his teeth and the pain duly subsided, leaving him again with a feeling of popping, bristling light-headedness. Above everything else Arm was tired. He watched the widow bodily address a sturdy, thigh-high drawer by the bed. She leant down against an edge of the drawer and shunted it sectionally out of place to reveal behind it, in the wall, embedded in the actual plaster, a small black rectangle. The widow opened the top drawer of the displaced dresser and rooted for a moment, fishing out a small key set. She isolated a key and inserted it into the black rectangle. The rectangle swung open on hinges. From out of it she withdrew a long metal case. It was heavy, Arm deducted, as the widow clunkily guided the case onto the floor. She manoeuvred down onto her knees, using another key to open the case. The case was full of banded rolls of money. Lots of rolls, too many to quickly count, thirty, maybe more, and some coins, and other pieces of paper that were likely cheques or drafts, but mostly hard cash, notes and notes, held together in thick folds by rubber bands.

'Over here,' Arm said.

He gestured and the widow took up a roll and handed it to him. Arm uncinched the band and the notes sprang open. The distinctive weathered smell of paper currency hit his nostrils. Arm snatched a tenner and held it close. A tenner, but it was coloured in green and brown, and then Arm noted the pound sign imprinted in its corner; it was not ten euro, it was ten Irish pounds. Arm flipped through the other tens. They were all pounds.

'This is old money,' he said.

The widow was still on her knees in front of him, a hand resting absently, familiarly, on his knee. This disquieted him. Her hand was still cold. The widow said nothing.

'This is pounds,' Arm went on, 'this is no good. This money's gone. It's done.'

'It's all there is,' she said, 'take it all off away with you,' and she offered him another banded bundle of pound notes. Arm went to stand up, fell forward onto his knees. Now the widow was over him, her hands on his shoulders.

'Steady. What are you at now?'

'I'm getting out of here. Hands off me.' Arm was piling the notes back into the case. He closed the lid and hefted the case under his arm.

'You're in no fit state for anything. Lie back down,' the widow said.

Arm pointed the hammer at her.

163

'Downstairs. Come on.'

Hector was still on the sitting-room floor, umoving. Arm loped in and bent to his body. He slapped the man's thighs, dug a hand into the pockets of his trousers, chanting all the time, 'Don't move, don't move, don't move.' He carried back a set of keys to the widow, standing in the hall.

'Let's go,' Arm said.

'Where?' the widow said.

'You're taking me home.'

It seemed like hours later when Arm woke again, a dried sweat on his forehead. The case of dead money was angled across his lap, and beside him in the driver's seat the widow stared implacably ahead with both hands fixed on the Hiace's steering wheel. Sounds of grinding metallic protest drifted up out of the depths of the van as they trundled along a lightless road. Arm looked out the side window. The night sky looked like something precious and crystalline had been smashed repeatedly against it.

'We on the right track?'

'It's a hospital we need to get you to, not home,' the widow said.

When Arm said nothing she said, 'I know this country. I have not driven in a long time and I have not ever driven a vehicle as burly as this contraption, but I know this country.'

'Just land me where I say. The town and that's it.'

'There'll be trouble,' the widow said. 'Home's the first place they'll find you.'

'Don't mind any of that.'

'A doctor, at least, Douglas, it will—'

'No.'

'You have to think of the others,' the widow said.

'What others?'

'The people in your life. Your family, Douglas. They will want you around.'

Arm's head was burning. He pressed it against the glass of the passenger window. To shut her up he said, 'I don't give a fuck about anyone but myself.'

'Now I don't think that can be true at all, Douglas,' the widow said, 'not at all.'

When Arm again refused to respond, the widow continued.

'I had a brother who died, in the end, of stubbornness. This was almost fifty years ago now. Tommy. My father kept horses, and Tommy used to break them in. He was the second oldest in the family, twenty-two, and I was the youngest, only eight at the time. One day Tommy came back in from the paddocks and into the kitchen as pale as a sheet, straw in his hair and on his clothes. Bewilderment in his eyes. My mother asked him what had happened and he was embarrassed, initially, to explain, but eventually admitted that a colt had managed to fall over on top of him. He'd been leading it around the paddock by a tether, one of the big, distemperate beasts, and in the business of restraining it the colt had somehow dropped down sideways on top of him, flattening him right into the ground. Tommy was shook and drawn, but he wouldn't hear of seeing a doctor. He was a strapping lad. He trotted in his boots around the kitchen and sat down at the table. He was grimacing a bit, but he seemed otherwise fine, so I suppose my mother believed him when he said he was okay. To prove his health he asked for a glass of milk, gulped it down, wiped his mouth with the back of his hand and just sat there and chatted away, about what I don't even remember, just the local gossip with my mother as she was making the dinner. Then he said he might go for a lie down. This wasn't unusual as he'd been up since before six and the evening was coming on. Tommy went in to his room and a little while after I took a notion and went in after him. He was staring up at the ceiling, blanket to his neck. His lips were white and they were stuck to his teeth, but his eyes were open. I asked him was he feeling okay and he continued to insist he was fine, just tired, though by now my mother had considered matters again and was making plans to get the doctor. But it was too late. Tommy just dropped off into a sleep, and he did not wake up.'

Presently the widow saw the lights of Ballintober approaching. With a neat satisfaction, she eased the boxy, ponderously responsive vehicle into the forecourt of the petrol station. She cut the engine and stepped down into the cool of the night and walked across the empty street, into the only building that appeared open. A few minutes later she emerged, followed by a heavyset man in black and an older man with a stagger in his walk and coloured fishhooks threading his angling jacket. The widow maintained a tactful distance ahead of the men as she led them across the road and opened the Hiace door. The man in black stood back while the man in the angler's jacket ventured a look inside. He was in wellingtons, and shifted his feet on the loosely pebbled macadam and leaned frankly in. He drummed his fingers evenly against the metal of the door and after what seemed a long time turned to the widow and told her that she was absolutely right, that the poor creature inside in that van was dead.

DIAMONDS

I left the city with my connections scorched and my prospects blown, looking only for somewhere to batten down for the winter to come. I left on a bright morning in August, dozing fitfully as the train drifted through the purgatorial horizontals of the midlands, heading west. The midland skies were huge, drenched in pearlescent light and stacked with enormous chrome confections of cloud, their wrinkled undersides greyly streaked and mottled, brimming with whatever rain is before it becomes rain. Each time I came to and checked the carriage window the same cow seemed to be eyeing me from the same sodden, tobacco-brown field. Or each cow bore the same expression; the huge jaws mechanically working a wad of cud back and forth, the dark eyes registering me with the same steady, sullen incuriosity.

I was not well. I was drinking, too much and too often, and had resolved to stop. In the city I had drank away my job, money, a raft of friendships, one woman, and then another. My cat, a princely tortoiseshell tom named Ruckles, succumbed to a heart attack after eating a phial of damp cocaine he'd unearthed at the bottom of my closet while I was out on another all-night jag. Ruckles's passing got me to thinking, in a vague and wistful way, of dying by my own hand. I began to consider my hands in the starlight of barrooms—the brittle wrists and yellowed skin, the nicks and weals and livid pink burn marks of unknown origin—and realised I was already way along on that project. It was go home or die, and home was an oblivion that was at least reversible.

I was thirty-three and had no extant family in the town. My parents were in the cemetery, my only sibling, an elder sister, moved to the States years back, and those locals who were once my friends were now grown strangers. It was my old secondary school principal who saved me. The principal was of a type, the Sentimental Authoritarian, who have always proven susceptible to my charms. Recalling my teenage athletic prowess—I had been the star of the football team, driving Saint Carmichael's boys to three successive provincial finals and winning two—he found me a sinecure as groundskeeper and part-time gym teacher. He had seen a talent burgeon under his institution's aegis, and did not want to think it truly snuffed out. I admitted I had come into this low ebb entirely of my own accord, but he assured me in time I could make things right.

I was billeted in a small cottage on the school grounds, and granted a modest stipend in exchange for executing my duties and staying sober. As groundskeeper I was tasked with keeping hale the clutches of flora decorating the institutional hillocks, ensuring the dumpsters were emptied on time, unlocking the gates in the mornings and keeping watch as the train of kids moiled in. I cut my hair neat and dressed in long sleeves, to conceal the tattoos that wound like black foliage down my arms. I carried a large, old-fashioned ring of keys and jingled them as I patrolled my appointed territories, advertising my approach to any boys risking a smoke in the bushes. In the school's evening emptiness, seeking some kind of cosmic reparation for Ruckles, I fed the stray cats that foraged about the skips, and in turn they brought me blood tributes, depositing on my cottage doorstep the tiny mauled carcasses of baby birds.

I taught gym a dozen hours a week. Gym was easy; the boys liked the class because it was only technically a class. I refereed games of indoor soccer and volleyball from a sideline deck chair and had only to blast the whistle if things became excessively robust. The boys not sportily inclined I designated 'stewards' and left to their own devices at the back of the hall, reading comics or catching up on homework, so long as one of them threw the ball back when it went out of play. I unrolled long, hortatory riffs at the fat kids as they heroically inched up the climbing ropes, and I came almost to cherish the swampy funk of perspiration the boys shed as they disported.

The Sentimental Authoritarian put me in touch with the local AA, a small and hardy group of sick-of-their-own-shit degenerates who met once a week in the town's Catholic church hall. Beneath fluorescent lights we recited the tales of our interminable fucking up. I listened and I talked and I listened and I talked, and I kept going back.

Winter came with a vengeance, as they say. The season felt like that, like a long, hard reprisal, exactingly meted. Snow whipped down in record quantities. The temperatures bottomed out, and the fallen snow stayed on the ground even as more fell. At night, the town river iced over in sections that came creakingly apart at dawn and floated downstream in jagged, table-sized panes. Cars fretted along at fifteen miles an hour on the high street and helplessly butted grilles. Now and then a lone pensioner was found frozen to death in their refrigerated council flat. I salted the lanes and macadam paths of the school, but every day a kid fell and pranged a knee or sprained a wrist. The stray cats died off and when the roads became impassable, the rubbish sat uncollected in frozen piles in the dumpsters, but no matter what I kept going to AA.

She showed up the first Sunday evening in December.

Mellick, the elder of our group, was up top, talking. The rest of us faced him, pitched and slumped in informal rows on foldaway chairs. The hall was large and bare. Along one wall was arranged a table bearing canisters of coffee, a bag of disposable plastic cups and a plate of inedibly stiff ham triangle sandwiches. Three ancient radiators clanked and burbled along the wall. Overhead, the ceiling lights buzzed, low and insinuating as a defect of the inner ear.

Mellick was seventy. He had drunk for fifty years and been clean, now, five. He was short three fingers and looked like what he was, a survivor. Like many survivors he held himself up as his own worst example. He was telling us again about the fingers. As he talked, he held his maimed right hand in his undamaged left. Where index, ring and middle finger should be, there were only the abrupt drumlins of his knuckles, the scar tissue whited over. I was up in the first row, looking right into Mellick's elongated, pitted face. I could see the battered horseshoe of his bottom row teeth, pocked with black metal fillings and rufous with rot.

She was sitting to my left. She was pale, wrung-eyed, copying unconsciously or not Mellick's arrangement of hands; one held in the other, fingers curled round showing bitten nails coloured with chipped blue nail polish. She was hunched over in her chair—head low, shoulders tucked in and braced—as if awaiting a blow to the nape. She was breathing through her mouth, eyes fixed to Mellick as he unpacked his old story.

Mellick was forty-one when he lost the fingers, he said. He was in a shed on his farm, shearing planks of timber while drunk, drunk and angry, why he can't remember, of course. He said he was hurling the lengths of wood into the spinning bandsaw, splinters going everywhere, into his hair and mouth and eyes, the blowbacking sawdust rendering him practically blind, when hand met saw.

It was over in an instant, Mellick said. Before he knew what had happened he was staring at the pumping red mess of his hand. Mellick said he had no idea how many fingers were gone; the spewing blood and the luminosity of the pain made it impossible to get a tally straight in his head. The pain, he said, was like a presence, a separate body or entity, standing there in the shed with him. He was scared, staggering around, looking for however many fingers he could find and getting rapidly woozy, knowing this wasn't a good sign, dazedly combing the straw and shaving-matted floor and all the time convinced he was going to bleed to death. And he did pass out, but he did not die, and by the time anyone knew what had happened the family cat (oh, Ruckles!) had already found the three severed fingers, eaten one until it was just a spur of bone with a nail attached by a thread of gristle, and stolen off with the other two.

'And did I learn anything from this experience?' Mellick asked.

Nobody said anything. I finicked with the cuffs of my shirt, crooked my head and brought the woman into my peripheral field. She was my age, maybe, early thirties, maybe younger, depending on the degree of damage she'd inflicted upon herself.

'I was back on it the second I was out of the hospital,' Mellick answered. 'It didn't so much as dent my appetite. Not for years, not for years, not for years.'

He cracked a mirthless smile. I did too. For this was what we were here for, the hardscrabble tutelage of those come out the other side of their damage.

The meeting over, a few of the Anons hovered by the coffee table, husking themselves into their jackets. There was motiveless chatter about the weather. After an hour of intensive gut spilling, it was nice to impersonate normal people.

'Excuse me,' she said to me.

Her hair was a wan, unconvincing brown; one prompt spook away from turning completely grey. She had a round face, pale eyes and a faded scar on her nose, a blanched diagonal seam, neat, across the bridge, like a tiny rope burn. She was not good-looking, but there was a watery indefiniteness to her features, a pliancy, that just then appealed.

'You're Carmichael's gym teacher, aren't you?'

I winced but admitted I was.

'Siobhán Maher. My boy is in your class. Anthony. He's a second year.'

I didn't say anything and she added, redundantly, 'I'm his mother.'

'Right.'

'I didn't know—I mean I don't know if you're allowed to say you know each other here?' she said.

'It's supposed to be anonymous.'

'That's not really practical around this ways, is it though?'

'I guess not.'

'This is my first time,' she said.

We stepped outside, into the bright white furnace of cold. I cupped my hands and blew. The hall was at the northern end of the church grounds. The church steeple, lit from below, loomed above a row of skinny elms. The snow had frozen into sparkling crusts upon the roofs and bonnets of our parked cars.

'Anthony's not the sportiest, I imagine?' she said, trailing me as I crunched my way to my car.

I thumbed the serrations of my car key's teeth and tried to picture Anthony Maher, summoning up a quiet, pale, heavyset boy who did not stand out in any way. The others called him Anto, but even that generic diminutive—suggesting a lad possessed of a rudimentary streak of devilment or impishness or participatory vim—did not suit the ponderous, frumpy boy I had to verbally goad into an amble in the rare games of five-a-side he consented to partake in.

'He holds his own,' I lied.

I opened the driver door. A lock of snow crumbled down and shattered on the seat. The car was a rickety secondhand number the Sentimental Authoritarian had sourced for me. Its previous owner was a priest and former Carmichael's faculty member, and the interior retained a smell I could only describe as *holy*, an aroma at once cloying and lightly sulphurous, redolent of thurified smoke or incense. It was a smell I could not eradicate no matter how much I scrubbed at the upholstery with solvents and sprays. Months later and it still made me gag.

When I looked up she was still there, standing by the taillights.

'Are you okay?'

'It's a cold one, isn't it?' she said, like that was an answer.

'You could get in.'

She slid into the passenger seat, into the fretwork of shadows thrown by the limbs of the elms.

'I just live in Farrow Hill estate. If it's on your way.'

'It is alright.'

I turned on the engine and let the car tremble warmingly in place, then nosed us out onto the main road. I

drove in second, mindful for black ice limning the macadam. There were long rumpled drifts of frozen snow
choking the ditches, their ridges sooted with exhaust.
Between us there was no talk for a little while, and there
still wasn't when she dropped her right hand on my leg
and began kneading my thigh, pressing slow and hard,
wincing and unwincing her fingers.

'How long have you been going?' she said.

'Where? To the meetings? Five months, give or take.'

'And you've been good all that time?'

'Not all that time,' I admitted.

'Was it just drink?' she said.

'Mainly,' I said. 'There was everything at some point.'

'And you were away before?'

'In the city.'

'And what did you do there?'

'This and that.'

'What kind of this and that?'

'Bars. Clerking. The sites. Played in a band. Barwork
was the best. Steady pay, all the drink you could drink
on the sly. You could go a long time lying to yourself in
there.'

'And now?'

'Now, I do what you said. I teach gym.'

'It's better,' she said.

'That it is,' I said.

We moved down Main Street, past the lights of the Turkish takeaway, the flayed loaves of chicken and pork
revolving on their spits in the window. We moved past
one, two, three pubs in a row, smokers outside, some

huddled, some affecting open-chested postures in defiance of the scouring subzero cold. I saw the drink in their faces, in the fuggy glower of their blood-bright expressions.

She directed me on to the quay road and we followed the river, a slash of brightness against the murk of the surrounding land. The water was freezing over again, growing scales.

'Carmichael's up ahead,' she announced.

'Uh-huh,' I said, and wondered if she knew I lived there.

On the riverside footpath, coming towards us, were two short figures. The boy on the inside had a scarf wound over the bottom half of his face, his hands in his jacket pockets, moving purposefully against the cold. The boy on the outside was not in so good a shape, tromping along with a pronounced crabwise stagger, listing to his left for three or four steps then lurchingly correcting. I looked again at the second boy and realised that the stocky, dough-faced features were those of Anto Maher. He was hammered, his face and head bared to the elements, his jacket unzipped and his trousers soaking wet from the knees down.

'Oh Christ,' she said. Her hand jumped from my thigh.

'There's your guy,' I confirmed.

'Him and that other eejit, Farrell,' she said, 'partners in crime.'

There was a section of waste lot, not far from the school grounds, some of the boys used for knacker drinking. I figured they were coming from there.

'You want me to stop?' I asked.

'No, no,' she said. 'This is what boys do, right? He tells me he's staying over at Farrell's house, watching DVDs and playing video games, and no doubt Farrell gives his mother the same shit.'

In the dark, and given Anto's condition, there was little chance that either boy would recognise me or my car or my passenger, but I stared straight ahead as we passed them.

'Take care of yourself, you dope,' she said in a low voice.

'Who's he more like?' I said. 'You, or his father?'

'Both,' she said. 'Luck will knock you only so far from the tree.'

'And where's the father now?' I asked.

'Oh,' she sighed. 'He's a thousand miles from here.' She laughed as she said this. 'No. Literally. He works in a mine in Africa, sorry, Siberia now, as big as any on earth.'

She looked across at me, still grinning.

'It's a huge hole in the ground that goes down almost a straight mile. You could pick up and drop this entire town into it in one piece. He comes back twice a year.'

'How's that suiting you?' I said.

'He's a good man for the couple of weeks he's around,' she said. 'He's a good man for the small doses. But remind me to show you a picture of the mine. It is something.'

'What are they after?'

'Diamonds,' she said.

'A mile down,' I said. 'It must get hot.'

'Left here . . . and a right.'

We slid into an estate, crested a hill. 'Here,' she said. I parked in the driveway. She said nothing as she got out. Beneath the porch light she held her handbag up close to her face and foraged for her keys. When she stepped inside she left the door ajar. I followed her in.

'What about you?' she said. 'You on your own?'

'I am.'

'Left a girl in the city?'

'Something like that,' I said.

We moved down the dark hall, into the kitchen.

She opened the fridge and a rhomboid of chilled light spilled across the floor, revealing a kitchen island, a table with two chairs pried back from it, as if the previous occupants had bolted from the seats in a hurry.

'Hi, moggy,' she said, and a cat, white coat splashed with black, emerged from a shadowed corner and dabbed across the tiled floor.

I took a chair. The cat slid in under my feet and commenced grinding its tiny weight against each chair leg.

'I think it likes me,' I said.

There was the heavy resonant thunk of a full bottle on the counter of the kitchen island. She unscrewed the cap, poured a long measure, and gulped it down. I could smell the whiskey. My heart began to race, as if I'd glimpsed the averted face of an old lover on a crowded street. She poured again. She shucked off her jacket, let it fall to the floor the way kids do. She came on over, the bottle in one hand, the glass in the other. I didn't wait for her to offer the drink—I spared her that—snatching the glass from her hand and downing it in one go.

'They must rate you in the school,' she said.

'It was a kindness, the job. I played football back when Carmichael's won stuff, and, you know, I was good. The old man didn't forget.'

'When I was in the convent, me and the girls would go down and watch some of the Carmichael's games, back when the Sisters still let us. Maybe I saw you play,' she said.

She was standing between the V of my legs. I returned the glass to her possession then rested my hand on the jut of her jeaned hip. She filled the glass again.

'I remember that,' I said.

The Sentimental Authoritarian had come up with the idea, and his equivalent number in the convent had consented to it. The idea was to expand local support, and so each game day a bunch of convent girls were bussed down to the grounds, bearing class-made banners in the Carmichael's and Convent colours. The girls were tightly chaperoned, of course, but every boy in Carmichael's staggered around in a humpbacked fever at the fact that live actual females were being permitted inside the school gates.

'Did you like it?' she said.

'I was good at it, so I guess I did.'

'I wonder if I noticed you,' she said. 'One of us probably did. We thought we were American high schoolers, in love with the quarterbacks.'

'I had best friends I saw every day for five straight years I wouldn't know now if I passed them in the street,' I said. 'So I won't be offended if you don't remember me.'

'But you were there and I was there,' she said. 'In our young skins, though we didn't know each other from Adam. Strange to think of it.'

'It was a long time ago.'

'Does it feel like that?' she said.

'How could it not,' I said. I curled the three middle fingers of my right hand into my palm, and waggled the thumb and baby. 'But what did you make of Mellick?' I asked.

'That terrified old cunt.'

'He's meant to be inspiring.'

'I don't want to end up like that,' she said.

I uncurled my fingers and reached for her hair.

In the upstairs bedroom, she flicked on a lamp.

'See.'

Tucked into the frame of her dresser mirror was a yellowing picture. The mine. I was expecting a photograph by or featuring Anto's father, but it was only an image from a paper or magazine. The picture was full colour, with a column of text in a foreign language occupying the upper left corner of the page. The photo had been taken from altitude, not directly overhead but high enough to encompass the entire circumference of the mine, which was, quite literally, a big hole in the ground. There was a town, or at any rate a stretch of dinky building-like structures, spread out along its far rim. The surrounding landscape was suitably desolate, a lunar terrain of chalks and greys and indeterminate formations of rock and dirt, scrubbed clear of anything alive or green. The mine was widest at the surface and narrowed as it deepened, like a funnel. Carved along the exposed inner strata of the mine wall was a presumably machine-made channel or pathway that wound all the way down to its unseen centre.

'It's big,' I said.

'And far away,' she said.

She knocked the light off, took my elbow and brought me to the bed. We undressed, and made an obligatory stab at fucking, our strivings ruddled by the whiskey. After, we sprawled in the foamy folds of the duvet and finished off the bottle. The whole time, I kept a portion of my attention perched out on a little ledge in the very back of my mind, straining for the telltale slam of the front door, the thunderous clomping of feet on the stairs, but the rooms beneath us were as still as the bottom of a lake.

'So is this a thing you do?' I said. 'Go to meetings, pick up someone you scent the weakness in?'

'I want to be better,' she said. '*He* was worse, a real demon for it, and *this* was the only way to live with him,' she said, wagging the empty glass. 'And then he went away, as far away as he could get. He said it was the only way any of us would get better.'

'And is it? Better?'

'It's something you only do to yourself, they're right about that,' she said. 'But I guess it's worse if there's someone else. And then there's Anthony.'

'He'll make it,' I said.

'Maybe he will.'

There was nothing else to say or do so I leaned in and kissed her, chastely, on the cheek. She traced her finger around the rim of the glass, dabbed the finger to her lips, kissed away the last amber fleck of whiskey, then turned away. After a while I got up and quietly dressed. I made my way downstairs, shoes in hand. Coming off the final stair step, I stumbled and brought my knee down on some sort of glass fixture—something that tinkled as it shattered. I hobbled down the hall, stuck my feet in my shoes, and let myself out. The dead-of-night cold was of a purity that scorched my lungs as I sucked it in.

The next morning, a Monday, I rose at seven. I bundled myself into my drab olive overcoat, loaded a double handful of council-issued road salt into my pockets and crunched down to the front gates, scattering the salt ahead of me as I went. I felt good, despite the familiar tightening in the midsection of my face that would bloom into a full-blown headache as the day wore on. I unlocked the gates, though the first of the kids would not show up for another hour. I went across the road, onto the riverside path. The sky was lavender, and there was a bank of high white clouds moving in off the Atlantic as stately as glaciers. I decided to walk up the town for a coffee and paper.

Passing the station I saw a bus about to depart. I asked the driver where to. It wasn't far, a little farther on down the west coast, but I hadn't been to that particular city in years. I had enough cash on me for a ticket and clambered on. In the city I ransacked my ATM card and checked into a small hotel off the high street. They asked for a name and I gave them a name, reversing the natural slant of my cursive as I wrote it out. I drank at the hotel bar, and in the afternoon did a circuit of the high street pubs. I did the same thing the following day. In the seclusion of the bars I felt like a ghost becoming slowly corporeal again.

I considered the lay of the land. It was easy to pick out the chronic soak-heads from the tourists, the amateur drinkers. It had something to do with the way they conformed themselves to the planes of the bar, the way they aggressively propped an elbow and periodically lifted a haunch from their stool to get the blood flowing back into that leg. It had something to do with the way they every so often softly exclaimed or sighed or rebukingly clicked their tongue at nothing and no one. The way they stared down into the weathered grain of the counter, mulling their special soak-head grievances and depletions. The way they were invariably alone.

The city was right up on the Atlantic. I walked the quays, the convoluted knot of cobbled alleys that wound narrowly back and forth through the tight parcel of buildings that constituted the city centre. There were strings of festive lights everywhere, council employees in high-viz jackets and wool caps scrubbing sleet into the drains with cartoonishly large black-bristled brooms. There were swarms of shitfaced stags and hysterical hens, and masked artists draped in tinfoil smocks impersonating statues in the street—even the cold could not disturb their poised inertia. My mobile filled up with voicemails, several from the Sentimental Authoritarian's secretary, and finally one from the man himself. His voice was mild and measured, shot through with a gorgeous note of presidential weariness. He was sure this was all some simple misunderstanding. He told me to ring just to let everyone know how long I'd be gone. He said to take care. At some point the battery of my phone died.

On the second or third or eleventh day I met a blond woman with a black tooth—a cap that hadn't taken and become infected. In lieu of small talk she immediately embarked on a lengthy diatribe against a man she referred to only as The Spider. She said he was a coward and selfish and probably a sociopath; a spiteful, petty bully congenitally incapable of empathy for others, though he was a *charmer* of course. He collected women this Spider and left his brand upon them—she pushed back her hair and angled her head. A perfectly lifelike blue arachnid was tattooed just under her ear.

'He made me get that,' she said, and she insisted there were over a hundred women in this wretched city bearing such a mark.

In my hotel room she scooped out her left tit and told me to say goodbye to it. She said it was riddled with tumours and was going to have to go. She said she almost certainly only had months to live. She saw me looking at her hair—it was bleached nearly white, and looked crispy in a dead way, like straw, but it was her real hair. She touched it self-consciously and said the doctors had assured her chemotherapy was pointless at this stage. I told her I was sorry, and she said that was okay; that she was putting everything that was the past, all the years of useless shit, behind her, and living only for now, for the moment, and that I was a part of the moment, and I should feel good about that.

And then she wanted to know my story.

It was dusk. There were crushed cans, empty miniatures and bottles littering the floor, stains soaked into the carpet, tangles of clothes. She was lying on the bed wearing nothing but my rumpled shirt. I was sitting in my underwear on the large wooden sill of the window. The radiators were on full blast and I had the window inched open.

I told her I was in town for just a few days, to check in on my ex-wife and kid, that I didn't get to see all that much of them anymore because I worked overseas as a diamond miner. She perked up at that.

'Diamonds,' she said.

She said I must make a mint and the next round of drinks was surely on me, so.

I nodded my head in a way that suggested that just might happen. She wanted to know about the mine and I told her it was basically just a huge hole in the ground, so big you could pick up this entire city and throw it down there in one piece. I told her it was mostly done by machines now, the actual mining, with the men only required to operate the machines at a relatively safe remove, but that it was still sapping and inhospitable work. I told her that with all the drilling and pounding, enormous quantities of dust and grit and dirt were churned up into the atmosphere, so much that sometimes the sun was almost blotted out, and that no matter how many filters or masks we wore, we were still breathing in a certain amount of that poisonous shit And there were of course the periodic on-site accidents, men getting injured, maimed, even killed. I told her how a good friend of mine, a tough old codger of a Ruski venerated as a legend by the other men, had lost three fingers on his right hand in an incident a few years back, and how now he had to make do with just a thumb and forefinger.

'Jesus,' she said.

'But then every line of living has its hazards,' I said kindly.

'Don't I know it,' she said, and yawned and stretched and settled herself again amid the pillows.

Then neither of us said anything and through the window I listened to the noise of another city, growing already familiar. I slid from the sill, put on my trousers and belt. I checked my wallet. I picked up my dead mobile, consulted its blank screen, and told her it was time to go.

KINDLY FORGET MY EXISTENCE

Owen Doran was sitting at the bar of The Boatman Tavern when his friend and former bandmate Eli Cassidy came through the door. By then Doran was the Boatman's sole visible occupant; shortly prior to Eli's entrance, Doran had witnessed the Tavern's barman, a monosyllabic Eastern European with a sharp-planed face, extravagantly scarred Adam's apple and skin-coloured crewcut, step into a trapdoor in the floor of the bar. The barman, hitherto a clipped, evasive presence, had raised a brow, established an instant of ferociously lucid eye contact, and dropped wordlessly out of sight.

Consigned so abruptly to his own company, Doran had felt exposed, on display. To stem his self-consciousness, he'd futzed with the extremities of his suit—pinching plumb his shirt cuffs and tamping securely under his chin the inexpertly folded knot of his tie. He had nipped restrainedly at his beer and tried his best to ignore the ticking of the clock above the bar.

When the Boatman's door thrummed on its hinges, Doran turned to the source of the disturbance bearing an instinctive scowl; seeing that the intruder was Eli, his scowl deepened out of sheer surprise. But then it occurred to Doran why Eli was there. Wiping at his face with his fingers Doran permitted himself a glance at the bar clock—it was, finally, gone eleven, and it was a relief to know it was gone eleven. He turned back to Eli and modified his craggy, pug-dog lineaments into an expression someone who did not know Owen Doran might mistake for benign.

'Welcome, fellow coward,' he drawled.

Eli Cassidy blinked and frowned in his dark coat. A residue of the rained-through morning had trailed him in and now it was diffusing from his hatless head and thin, sloping shoulders like a contagion.

'You on your own?' Eli said, shaking off his coat. Underneath, a black suit.

'The man will be back, he's just belowground a spell,' Doran announced. 'Drink?'

'Redundant question,' Eli replied, stalking forward.

Eli's rinsed brogues squeaked on the Tavern's floor-boards. He transferred his overcoat from one arm to the other. Limply piled and dripping, it resembled the lustre-less corpse of a drowned animal. Eli heaped the coat on the stool adjacent to Doran's, but remained standing himself. Eli looked good, a trim man in his forties in a well-cut suit, though Doran could detect the reek of tobacco beneath the crisp ozone scent of his wetness. And the suit, on second look, was not quite pristine; there were streaks and gobbets of something slick adhering to the trouser legs.

'Is that shit on your knees?' Doran asked.

Eli looked down.

'Just mud.'

'Did you fall?'

'Yes,' Eli admitted. His face mottling, Eli considered the row of bar taps, their black levers level in the air. A small vein throbbed above his right eye. 'I'll just wait for the fucking guy, I guess then,' he sniffed.

Doran sighed, fitted his feet against the lowest rung of his stool and levered himself halfway over the bar, gut pressing into the counter's bevelled edge. He eyed the trapdoor in the floor, its rectangular metal door yawning upward, resting at a forty-five degree angle against a shelf of soft drinks and no sign at all of the barman.

With no little dexterity, Doran contorted his right arm in under the bar, extracted a pint glass, and from his side of the counter pressed down a tap and held the glass angled in place as he evenly poured a pint. Doran watched in the bar mirror as the glass filled, as the pint's head bubbled and bloomed. Pouring from the wrong side of the bar required the same queasy narrowness of concentration as writing with your weaker hand.

'Well done,' Eli said as Doran handed him the pint. 'The staff don't mind?'

'What staff?' Doran said, looking around and snapping two fivers from his wallet. 'There's one post, and it's been abandoned.' He put the money by the taps.

'How are you, anyway?' Eli said.

'How am I? A tad dismayed to find I've as little a pair of balls on me as you.'

Eli took a mouthful of his pint. 'Psychic of you to have the same notion, alright,' he said.

'Cravens think along the same lines. Though I was here first,' Doran said, 'which makes me definitively the cowardlier.'

'You didn't go up at all then?' Eli asked, nodding towards the Tavern's windows.

Doran shook his head. His dirty red hair was gathered and cinched into a small, Samurai-ish pigtail at the crown of his head, and he had tidied up his beard, Eli noted. Doran was a short man with a barrel chest lapsing into a greedy boy's pot belly. He was wearing a cheap, boxy suit that was deep navy, not black, and his tie, unflatteringly wide and short, was patterned with what Eli now realised were tiny skulls. Such a flourish of gallows impudence was Doran's style alright.

'Did you?' Doran said. 'Go up?'

'I had a wander,' Eli admitted, low-voiced. 'The cemetery first. To see where they were putting her. It's on a hill.'

'Maryanne,' Doran said.

Eli gave a small shake of his head. The shake was not demonstrative; it was to himself. 'Maryanne,' he said. 'When did you hear?'

'A couple of days back,' Doran said. He looked at Eli. 'I'm sorry,' he said, with a formal wince of his brow.

'Me too,' Eli said.

'How's Laura?' Doran asked.

'She's good.'

'She know you're here?'

Eli shrugged.

'And the baba?'

'I refrained from sharing my plans with the three-year-old,' Eli said. 'You got any creature on the scene yourself?'

Doran grinned. 'Those days are done, I'm almost sure.' He splayed a hand on the counter and inspected the digits, as if in a moment of recent inattention a ring might have somehow contrived to snag itself there. 'No,' he continued, 'I've entered the era of grand onanistic solitude, and, to be honest, that's fucking fine by me.'

'I doubt that,' Eli said.

'Well,' Doran said, raising his brows and trailing diplomatically into silence.

Doran's eyes went again to the clock. Eleven minutes past eleven. The burial would follow at noon. He himself had arrived at the Tavern just after nine, empty-stomached but full of cringingly honourable intentions. His plan had been to bolster his courage with a quantity of preliminary drinks before heading to the funeral. But the drink had not coaxed forth that kind of courage (as he knew, in his bones, it would not), and so Doran had sat, and not moved, and eleven had come and gone, and he had kept drinking in order to tolerate his ingrained cowardice. Cowards were cowards, Doran considered ruefully, but they required conviction to be so—the brave thing was usually the easier thing.

Doran took a long draught of his pint and smacked his lips with satisfaction.

'Mortality's a skull-fuck, isn't it?' he said.

'Hm,' Eli grunted.

'She wasn't well,' Doran said, 'is what I heard.'

'Me too,' Eli said.

'Did we always know she was not well?'

Eli considered the skulls on Doran's tie, the repeating rows of black eyes.

'I don't know. You think on it, you turn things over. But the memories come out of your notions of them, what you thought was happening. And Christ knows we all had our dramatic days, back then. But if you're asking if I ever thought she'd do this . . .'

'It would never have occurred to me to ask,' Doran interjected, looking down into the sudsy, popping surface of his pint. 'Was it done violently, I wonder? Was there grisly theatre involved? A messy aftermath.'

'Christ, it hardly matters now,' Eli said.

'Or painlessly, hygienically,' Doran went on. 'There was a guy back in the day, and when I say day, I mean the forties. A writer. He done himself in and had to leave a note of course, had to attempt a pithy little addendum. "I am going to put myself to sleep for a bit longer than usual. Call it eternity," is how he signed off this planet.'

'You want to control it,' Eli said.

'Fuck her,' Doran said. 'Fuck her for what she did. And we're not even getting the worst of it, are we? We're the old guard. We're from the old way-back days. We've already had to get over her, haven't we?'

'Fuck her,' Eli repeated softly, experimentally. He turned composedly to the bar. He kneaded the bridge of his nose, the sockets of his eyes.

'Sorry,' Doran said.

'Why? You're just Doran being Doran,' Eli explained.

'*Sorry*,' Doran said again, 'you know my cuntishness is as congenital as my cravenness. The only cure is no me.' Doran extended a beefy palm, patted Eli's shoulder. 'But I was always glad you and her got together, you know.'

Eli chortled. 'Now that was a bad idea.'

'It was a fucking terrible idea,' Doran grinned. 'But what wasn't, back then? After I quit I spent a season licking the windows in the mother's house in Portlaoise, for instance. You two tried, anyhow.'

'The marriage was insanity.'

'The glory days,' Doran said wistfully. 'You say we had our moments but not you. You were a good boy for so long. Sensible, abstemious. You were, Eli, sorry, that sounds like an insult but it's not. Only she could turn you out of your equilibrium. She had a knack for it.'

'Not that she meant it, I don't think,' Eli mused. 'But she did make you want to lie down in the middle of traffic, alright.'

'Was that how it felt?' Doran asked.

'That's what it feels like it felt like,' Eli said. 'But I don't know. I don't know how it was for her. At all.'

Eli took a sip of his beer, Doran a deep quaff The bar man showed no sign of resurfacing; the clock ticked on. Eventually Doran gave a gentle, annunciatory clearing of his throat.

'She was our girl, a singer in our band, is what she was,' he said. He raised his glass and kept it aloft until Eli chinked it.

Eli could not deny that, at least. Sunken Figure was the band Eli, Doran, and a third friend, Proinsias Stanton, had founded in college, twenty years ago. Doran had been the original frontman and lyricist, ransacking undergrad poetry anthologies to flesh out the pornographic gibberish he half barked, half crooned. Eli wrote the actual music—clean post-punk lines and agitated percussion—and played bass. Stanton was lead guitar and for a time attempted to manage the band. Maryanne Watt first materialised on Stanton's arm, a serious girlfriend, in the long post-college epoch Sunken Figure spent toiling upon the capital's circuit. Stanton himself soon gave up, quitting the band for a job in the national forestry. Maryanne quit him and stuck with the band. Eli convinced Doran to let her on stage. And she did look good, rattling a tambourine and occasionally contributing tremulous backing vocals. Other members—drummers and auxiliary guitarists and keyboardists—came and went and Sunken Figure laboured amiably on, eking out enough of an existence to continually defer extinction, until the turn of the millennium, when something like actual success occurred. There was, finally, a major label deal, a hit single. There was coverage, attention, even money. And then came the grand folly: a marathon triple-figure-date tour that ate up thirteen months of their lives and killed Sunken Figure stone dead.

The trouble started with the single. For the major's album, *Ley Lines*, Maryanne had sung lead on only one song, a B-side that was shifted up onto the official track-listing at the last minute, but that song was the hit. Every interview and public appearance thereafter was an exercise in clarification. What the world wanted was more folk-pop gems smoulderingly essayed by the willowy

brunette—instead it got more Doran, howling and spit-
ting on his haunches over lengthy, bristling compositions.
The classic soap-operatics kicked belatedly in: at some
ill-advised point Doran and Maryanne began sleeping
together. The tour just would not stop. As things soured
Maryanne migrated from Doran's bed to Eli's. Eli had
been sadly, silently in love with her since the time he had
first laid eyes on her, and he gravely capitulated to what
could only be a bad idea. Neither were the affairs successive, but concurrent. In the panoptic confinement of tour
life Maryanne alternated nights with Doran and Eli.
Doran, surprisingly, was the one to quit first. With a
month left on the tour, he stole away on a dawn flight
from a frostbitten airport in Helsinki, made for the rural
midlands town he had sprung from and summarily
deposited himself into the care of his mother, to embrace
what he would thereafter denominate his Brian Wilson
period—a six-month interval of flannel-pyjama'd reclu-
siveness, weight gain, around-the-clock dope-smoking
and twilight bouts of compulsive weeping in the back-
yard greenhouse, the mildewed cord of his bathrobe
stuffed into his mouth to stymie the worst of his guttural
heaves.

Determined to salvage something from the implosion
of Sunken Figure, Eli and Maryanne got married. All
through his music career, sensible and stoic Eli had barely
drunk and studiously eschewed all harder substances,
but by the end of their connubial stint Eli's appetite for
illicit stimulants in general and cocaine in particular had
outpaced even Maryanne's, no mean feat. What money
did not go up their noses they fed into the production of

Maryanne's solo record, *In the Gardens of the Lune*, a dauntingly ambitious, sonically incoherent concept album that took as its subject matter the posthumous travails of a fictional family of dead Jews (Holocaust victims, naturally) residing as superpowered ghosts inside the moon. Over layers of wintry distortion, amateur-sounding instrumentation and time signatures so scrambled they practically induced nausea, the lyrics unpacked a labyrinthine downer of a narrative in which the family's little ghost son and ghost daughter commit ghostly incest, learn to manipulate the tidal patterns of the earth, and eventually cause the waters of the world to flood the entirety of Central Europe—all conveyed by Maryanne in an electronically treated, Bjorkesque fusillade of yips, shrieks and blurts. The album was not well received.

The marriage ended after fourteen months. Maryanne stayed on in London. Eli returned to Dublin. Doran, recovered from his fugue, showed up there too. Eventually the men crossed paths. There was awkwardness, but little animosity, and with Maryanne and Sunken Figure subtracted from the equation, they found making peace relatively easy. If they did not return, quite, to being friends, they were happy to let their orbits resistlessly overlap. Years passed. Eli became an accountant—he had a wife now, Laura, and a daughter. Incapable of any other life, Doran returned to the scene, scratching around with a couple of new bands, running DJ nights and picking up production gigs here and there. He became a sort of ironical eminence, courted by each new wave of local musicians ready to buy him a pint in exchange for a few war stories. But Doran seemed okay, to Eli, more or less functioning and more or less content, or contentedly discontent, and that was the best the likes of Doran was ever going to get. Meanwhile trickles of info regarding Maryanne made its way into Eli's ear. He heard she remarried, that she too had had a little girl. But nothing more substantive than those scant elementary updates, until this.

Doran said, 'I loved her too.'

'Yes,' Eli said.

He was looking at the windows. The rain had stopped. The inner panes of the windows were layered with dust; what light came through appeared microbial, quivering with impurities. The Boatman faced onto a lane that ran along one side of the cemetery wall. The cemetery gate was at the end of the lane. The procession, both men knew, would pass right by the pub. They would not be able to avoid seeing it, Eli realised, or at least making out its long, aggregated silhouette in those same dirty windows.

'I saw the family,' Eli declared.

'Oh?' Doran said.

'After I went up the hill I took a path down to the rear of the church. Curiosity, I guess. I hopped a fence and squinnied down behind a row of saplings. Hence the dirty knees. I hunkered down and watched through a bush, saw them going into the service.'

'On your knees?'

'So I wouldn't be seen.'

'Ah,' Doran said.

'I caught a glimpse of them, alright,' Eli said.

Over the totality of the years Eli had met Maryanne's father exactly once—a tense hotel dinner through which Eli suffered the thin, vertiginous feeling that everyone at the table, including himself, was being played by actors. Maryanne's father, a retired barrister, was even then implausibly elderly, eighty-six to his daughter's twenty-eight, though he was still hale and snappishly alert. The dashing woman in her fifties accompanying the father was very much not Maryanne's mother. The actual mother was purportedly insane, certifiably so, and had been domiciled in an institution as far back as Maryanne could remember, and that's all Eli ever got out of her about her mother. There was one sibling, an older brother who worked in Futures, in Hong Kong, and who never came home.

'Furtivity is our natural state,' she had told Eli when he asked why she always said so little about her family.

'I saw the father,' Eli continued. 'Must be touching a hundred now. In a wheelchair, flunkies either side. Insane. I saw the brother. Had to be him, looks just like her. A double, disconcerting to see her in a man's face. I saw—I think—the husband, and the kid, her girl. But they didn't see me. And they wouldn't know who I was if they did.'

'But they would know *of* you,' Doran said.

'Maybe,' Eli said doubtfully. He drained his drink. He put the glass down. He blinked, heavy-lidded. He was woozy after that single pint, and knew he would be on his ear if he went as far as three. He considered the door in the floor.

'He's down there? The guy,' he said. 'How long?'

Doran rubbed his chin. 'He must be in fucking China by now. Fuck this noise, this is negligence. You want another bev?'

Eli grimaced, considered his constitution, and said, 'Yes.'

'Hup,' Doran said, rising again over the counter and searching with his hand for more clean glasses.

'Eh, hi,' Doran heard Eli declare. Something moved in front of Doran. A package of refrigerated muscle encased his hand and commenced crushing his finger bones together. Doran looked up. The barman's smile loomed above him, mild and indicting, and beneath that smile a second one, lividly concertinaing his neck.

'No,' the barman hissed.

Doran wrenched his hand free of the man's pale grip.

'A word would've achieved the same,' he said, shaking his smarting hand in the air.

'Can't. Just. Take,' the barman said with infinite reasonableness. Then: 'What you want?'

Doran ordered the drinks and the barman picked out two clean glasses.

'What were you doing down there anyway?' Doran asked, nodding towards the door in the floor.

'Inventory.'

'Well now. That's as good an excuse as any. What's your name?'

'Dukic.'

'Do-kitsch?'

'Dukic.'

Eli watched the barman top up the pints and dip each in turn, tipping away the runoff. The sloughed foam pumped down the outside of each glass and sank into the grated metal recess under the taps. The barman was tall, six four at least. His scars were hideous, a row of ragged, mortified grooves bright against the lines of his collar.

'Well I'm Doran. And this is Eli.'

The barman gave an acknowledging grunt and distributed the pints, hooking away the empties in the same movement.

'This,' Doran said, and with his index finger circled his own Adam's apple. 'It's a nasty fucking razor burn, Do-kitsch. How'd you end up with it, if I may ask?'

The barman drew himself up. His lips twitched. He seemed to be deciding whether to say anything at all. Then he grinned, politely, as if he was obliged to find the reminiscence fond, 'I was in the war.'

'The war,' Eli said.

'Of course,' Doran said. 'And which one was that?'

'Bosnia. You recall?'

Doran waved a hand in the air. 'There was a bunch of them down that neck of the woods, wasn't there? Serbs, Croats, Sarajevans, all that noise, killing the shit out of each other.'

The barman nodded.

'I mean, it was complicated, so forgive my ignorance,' Doran said.

'It was not your problem,' the barman said.

'Though evidently, it was yours,' Doran said with some regret.

'Now just excuse,' the barman said and retreated deftly five feet down the bar. He stooped low, rummaged momentarily and returned to his full height brandishing a chequered blue-and-white terrycloth and a purple bottle of lemon cleaning spray. He turned a tap and ran the terrycloth beneath it, then twisted out the excess moisture. Onto the dark brown surface of the counter he dashed a succession of brisk, parallel jets of the lemon spray. He waited for the mist to settle before applying the damp terrycloth, bringing it in a neat rectangle around the sprayed section of the counter, then working inwards in diminishing, carefully nested rectangles.

'Now continue,' he said.

'With the interrogation?' Doran smiled. 'Sorry. We just need our minds taken off the here and now. We're drowning in morbidity here. You get a lot like us, I imagine, funeral-goers in their maudlin moods.'

The barman, eyes following the terrycloth, shrugged his shoulders. His English was good, but it was impossible to know how much of Doran's talk the man was following. Without looking up he said, 'We get everybody.'

Doran gripped the lapels of his suit, flick-wrenched them into tautness. 'But not us, not us,' he singsonged. 'So you were in the army then? In the war, in Bosnia?'

'Army. Yes. I was.'

'And that's when you got that collar?' Doran said.

The barman grunted again. He put away the cloth and spray, and travelled back up to the spigots. To Eli, he said, 'Your friend talks a lot of questions.'

'That he does,' Eli said, wondering if Doran was going to keep at the guy, and already knowing the answer. Something like fatigue swept over Eli; it would be his job to intercede, to referee or placate if Doran went too far with his escalating provocations, as he so often did.

'I'm just interested in the world. I'm an interested person,' Doran pleaded. 'You must forgive me in advance, like all my other friends,' and clapped Eli on the back.

The barman grinned again.

'It was friends did this,' he said.

'Friends?'

'Friends bombing friends. Our own men,' he raised a hand over his head and whirled it around, miming either falling ordnance or debris or both. 'Thinking we were not who we are.'

'Some friends,' Doran said. 'Jesus, huh?' He turned to Eli. 'Well, Do-kitsch is opening up now, though I couldn't prise two words out of him earlier.' He raised his glass to the barman. 'I'm sorry about your friends. But life goes on, huh? For us, at any rate.'

The barman smiled neutrally and tended to another task beneath the barline. Doran and Eli sipped their drinks. Eli looked to the windows again. It was becoming unbearable, the waiting. He felt a grainy runnel of dust in his throat and he could see, where the light was most acute, the motes scuffling in the bar's sealed atmosphere. He wanted air. He wanted a cigarette but he also wanted air.

'They'll be coming this way any minute now,' he groaned.

'Stay put. Keep the head down and stay put,' Doran said tightly, bolting what was left of his drink and whirling his finger for another.

'You are not going to your funeral?' the barman asked.

'Doesn't look like it,' Doran said.

'Why?'

'Ah, because we're scared,' Doran said.

'Scared,' the barman repeated, huffing amusedly through his nostrils.

'We're not,' Eli said, annoyed at Doran's insistence upon this point, even if it was true.

There was a lapse into silence, and Eli waited for Doran to fill the void. But it was the barman who spoke next.

'Well, I tell you,' he said, 'you made me a little strange when you come in?'

'Me?' Doran practically squealed with delight.

'Yes.'

'Why?' Doran asked.

'I tell you,' the barman said. 'You see you look like a man, exactly like a man I saw in the street. In the city, in the siege,' he said.

Doran looked at Eli then turned back to the barman.

'Good fuck, go on,' he demanded.

'This man, he was trying to get to a woman and child. This is with the shooting, the bombs, every day, all day. Snipers in their holes, up high. Shooting all day. The noise of the bullets whizzing and whizzing in the air. The woman and child—maybe his wife, his daughter? They were already gone. In the street.' The barman held his hands vertically out, palms facing each other, then pressed them in close. 'In a *thin* . . . ? *Alley*? One and one.' Now his fingers pinched adjacent spots in the channel he had shaped in the air, placing the little bodies. 'And after a long quiet time, he come out, running. To get them, this man, you see. Crazy. Running, but too slow. The bullets, whizzing, whizzing. And so,' a jerk of the shoulder, 'he is one of them too.' He pinched a final spot in the air, like he was quenching a candle. 'He look like you.'

'He look like me,' Doran cackled.

'Yes,' the barman said. 'This is why, when you come in . . .' he raised a finger to his temple, corkscrewed it, 'and I am back. I am there.'

'He haunts you,' Doran said.

'Who?' the barman said.

'The man, the man, the man who looked like me?'

'Ah!' The barman hyphenated his brow in reproof of such a notion. 'Nonono,' he smiled, 'I had forgot him. Like this,' he snapped his fingers. 'But you walk in today, and so he comes to me. It was a long time ago.'

He put out two more drinks.

'A long time ago,' Doran mused in a smooth, declaratory tone, as if he was about to start telling his own story. But all he did was scratch at the stubble on his chin.

'Yes. Now please excuse, I must—' the barman forked two fingers in front of his lips and mimed exhaling, then pointed to the door.

'I'll join you,' Eli said.

'You're going out there?' Doran said.

'It will be fine,' the barman said. 'Please, do not interfere again with the taps. I will be right back.'

Eli held the door. The barman strode through, so tall he had to duck to avoid the lintel. Doran watched them go over the rim of his glass.

Outside the sky was a dismal monochrome. The men arranged themselves side by side on the lane's narrow pavement in front of the tavern. The cemetery wall ran tall. There were trees on the other side, their thickly leaved and shadowed branches jostling above the stone. The barman was watching them. He had conjured already from somewhere a cigarette into his mouth. Unlit, he ignored it and stared fixedly ahead, his face in profile intent yet expressionless. In fact not a part of his body was moving; it was as if he had switched himself off. Such self-effacing stillness, Eli thought, must be a useful trait in a barman, who was after all only required to exist at specific intervals.

Eli nervously bumped a pack of cigarettes from his suit jacket. When he proffered a light the barman became abruptly animate again, turning to Eli with an appreciative grin. Eli lit them up, one and one. Wisps of smoke zipped away on a wind he could barely feel.

'I have a wife and child,' Eli announced.

'Yes,' the barman said tonelessly, as if this disclosure was to him a drearily familiar fact.

'Your story,' Eli went on. 'About the guy in the alley. His wife and kid. I have a wife and kid,' and felt instantly facile for having invoked the comparison.

The barman said nothing. He began to rock curtly to and fro on his heels, lending the impression he was shivering, although it was not unusually cold. He looked up the lane, down it, and then back at the trees; the smaller branches were in a state of continual minor agitation.

'It was a story,' the barman said finally, with flat finality. 'Your friend made me remember.'

'Were you the one shooting?' Eli said.

The barman looked at Eli's eyes; not into, but at. Eli considered the possibility that this man deserved his scars—deserved worse, perhaps—but how would you ever know? Balanced against the doubt that his grievous little anecdote was either entirely fabricated or so extensively embellished as to be practically fiction was the doubt that it was not.

The barman took a dainty drag of his cigarette—he was smoking with such hallucinatory slowness that Eli was beset by the misimpression his cigarette had not diminished at all—and held the smouldering cylinder towards Eli.

'I thank you for the light,' he said.

'That's alright,' Eli muttered.

Eli looked up, and beyond the barman's shoulder he saw them coming. The long-bodied, shining black hearse, flanked and pursued by its trail of mourners, all moving together at a stately crawl. The procession came down the lane. Eli stepped into the doorway of the Tavern as the hearse went by.

Maryanne's father, a grim wisp in a suit and wheelchair was at the centre of the group in immediate train behind the hearse. A pouting kid in her late teens had been assigned chair-pushing duties. A foreign-looking woman was holding the old man's hand and leaning over him with a health-care professional's solicitous disinterest as she paced carefully in step with the chair. There was the brother, paunchy, middle-aged but retaining an indelible vestige of Maryanne in his face. There and gone, and after him came the husband; at least ten years older than Maryanne, a bushy-browed man with a genteelly dissolute look to him, his cheeks rucked, a grey stripe running through his sandy hair. With his hands he was steering the shoulders of a little six- or seven-year-old girl. Eli knew who she was. Her face was mercifully veiled. None paid the least attention to the two men standing by the Boatman's entrance. The crowd's obliviousness filled Eli with relief, and made all his trepidation seem silly—for all this, he realised, had nothing to do with him.

When the last of the procession had passed, the door behind Eli opened. He felt something against his shoulder blade. It was Doran, grinding his forehead against Eli as zealously as a cat. Doran lifted his face, and turning around Eli saw that it was blotched.

'Ah, fuck it,' Doran said. 'Let's do this.'

'You're coming?'

'I always was. But if I start bawling, it's cos I'm three-quarters cut.'

Doran had brought his pint glass with him. He drained what was left and proffered the glass to the barman. The barman took it. Addressing Eli, he indicated with his smoking hand towards the receding procession.

'This is yours?'

'This is ours,' said Eli, dropping his cigarette onto the pavement and administering a summary stamp of his brogue as he stepped out into the lane. Doran followed. They soon caught up, and by the time the procession reached the cemetery entrance, the barman, still smoking and watching for nothing better to do, could barely distinguish the pair from the rest of the party, save for the substantial orange dot of the fat one's head.

The tall man and the fat man and the rest of the group passed through the gates and out of sight. The barman killed the cigarette and stowed the remainder in his pocket; no sense in wasting. When he went back inside he saw that the tall one had left his coat, lumped and dripping on a stool. It was a good coat, three-quarter length and nicely tailored, expensive, the barman saw once he unheaped it and wrung it out. He checked the pockets for identification, but found nothing. He hung the coat on a rack in the back room, scrolled up a couple of sections from an old Sunday paper, and stuffed the scrolls into each arm, dropping additional sheets of the paper on the floor beneath the coat to sop up any residual drippage, and waited for the man to return. An hour or so later a small band of mourners did drop in, but neither of the two men. The next morning the coat was still there, unclaimed. *Soon*, the barman thought, holding up another polished glass to the teeming, grained light that every day coursed through the Tavern's dirty front windows, *the man will come back for it*. But the man never did.

Acknowledgments

Thanks go to:

Declan Meade, Jonathan Dykes, Thomas Morris, Sean O'Reilly and Fergal Condon;

James Ryan, Éilís Ní Dhuibhne, Harry Clifton, Frank McGuinness, Susan Stairs, Claire Coughlan and Jamie O'Connell;

the Arts Council;

Lucy Luck;

Lucy Perrem;

the family.